The Ship

by

David Fabio

David Fabio

Photographs by David Fabio

Contents

List of Characters

Agent Mark Lawson – FBI

Agent Olson - Customs

Jackson Smith – DEA

Art Swenson – Wisconsin DNR

Alex North – Deputy Lake County Sheriff's Department

Rick Bernaski – Douglas County Sheriff

Agent Farley – Homeland Security

Bo Callahan – Dead man

Captain Taccetta – Captain of the Calvin Wroth

Joe Labonta – 2nd Mate

Leo Brasso – 3rd Mate

Stubby O'Shea – Crewman

Swede – Able Seaman

Blackie – Engineer

Eric – Cook's helper

Paul Radcliff – Electronics engineer

Agent Olson – Minneapolis Customs Agent

Kyle Easton – New Jersey ICE

Roy Hacket – New Jersey FBI

Kim Chang-Sun – North Korea

Duri Sol Ju – North Korea

Introduction

Law enforcement is a challenging field. Even for the seasoned field agent, cases tend to take surprising directions just when you thought you had them figured out.

Occasionally, you run into an interesting story that you keep telling yourself, someone ought to write this one down. They are the cases that make the job interesting. Well, this is one of those stories.

Law enforcement agencies attempt to work together to solve many of the most difficult cases. Without the whole picture, it is hard for the public to understand how the individual cases might be related to each other.

This was one case that cooperation almost didn't happen.

From the files of Special Agent Mark Lawson - FBI.

Chapter 1

The Hunt

The morning was a picture perfect day for hunting pheasants.

A gentle morning's cool breeze was quickly being replaced by the sun's bright radiance, which upon being absorbed by the soon to be harvested crops, was gently warming up the fields.

Our hunting group consisted of Wisconsin DNR Agent Art Swenson, Minnesota Lake County Sheriff's Department Deputy Alex North, and myself - FBI Special Agent Mark Lawson.

We gathered to attest to our shooting skills, in the fields of northern Wisconsin, after one of our joint law enforcement meetings.

During one of our meetings, DNR Agent Swenson suggested the outing. Because of his knowledge of the area, he would be acting as our personal director of the hunt. We decided that each one would drive our own cars to a small town in the area where we were planning to hunt, so we could head back to our homes directly from there.

Once we arrived at the selected location, we could all jump in Agent Swenson's car, allowing him to guide us to the golden fields where the pheasants were waiting.

The drive would take us about an hour south of Superior, Wisconsin to a set of cornfields in the area where Art Swenson grew up. He was still close friends with all the current owners of the farms. The fields in the area that had been planted with beans had been harvested, but the cornstalks were still standing tall. They wouldn't be harvested for a few weeks, while the corn was drying on the stalk.

The only thing our group was missing was a trusty dog to spot the birds hiding in the field. Art's hunting dog, a 13-year-old golden retriever, had died a few weeks earlier, and with our last minute planning, it did not leave him time to borrow a hunting dog from one of his friends.

The bright, cloudless sunlight would be an advantage to the hunters in spotting the birds as they ran between the cornstalks. The sunlight on the radiant plumage of the pheasants would stand out. At the same time, anyone duck hunting in the area would have hated the bright sunlight. It would have chased the ducks high in the sky, out of the reach of their shotguns.

After putting on some well-worn orange safety vests that DNR Agent Art Swenson had kept stored in his vehicle, he then gave each of us each a 12-gauge shotgun Art had brought from his own collection, just for the occasion.

The orange safety vests would help us spot each other in the tall corn, as the group spread out and walked the rows looking for the elusive birds.

This year, the stalks of corn were over seven-foot tall, making hunting difficult.

It was especially tough on Deputy North, as she was only five foot six. The birds definitely had the advantage.

Even for the slightly taller guys, the tall corn would create a challenge. If the bird was in front of you along the cornrow, it was an easy shot. However, if you had to swing your gun to the side, corn tassels would be flying with each and every shot.

Without a good dog to spot and pin them down, the pheasants could easily out-run their adversary or simply hide in the rows between the hunters.

We started our hunt at the north end of one of the fields. We were almost to the end of the first field before we spotted the first bird take flight. It was smart enough to stay low to the corn making a good shot over the cornstalks almost impossible.

"Hey, Mark, I thought one of you was going to call the bird and get off a good shot. What happened?" Art asked. "I thought that bird was in your direction."

"I thought it was ladies first," I jested.

"Sorry, I would have taken the shot, but I would have had to shoot it over your heads," Alex shouted back. "Actually, I really was hoping to see if you could catch a falling bird, or if you would simply duck."

Alex was a lot more interesting than I thought she would be. Usually, most of the female officers were rather strict and to the point. It was fun to see that she had a sense of humor.

After walking the entire field and getting off only one errant shot, our group decided to try another field, which was located closer to a marsh. Art was hoping the birds would be hanging closer to the edges of the corn, allowing us to get a better shot if they flew out towards the marsh.

The next field, where Art knew the owner, was less than a mile away. As we drove down the gravel road that led to the field, I spotted something, and pointed up the road.

"What do you think? Are those crows or ravens up ahead in the ditch?" I inquired.

We could see that there were several dark birds in the ditch on the left, about a block ahead. It probably meant there was either some road kill in the ditch that they were picking on, or one of the farmers had spilled some of their harvested corn or beans. Either way, whatever it was, it was fair game for the birds.

As we got closer, Art Swenson slowed down and stopped.

"Sorry, Mark, those aren't crows or ravens, those are eagles," he informed me, as one of the white-headed bald eagles left the group and headed toward the closest tree.

We sat and watched closely as a group of eagles had obviously been picking the remains of something on the side of the road. Slowly, the eagles started to become aware that they were being observed.

One by one, they flew off to one of the nearby trees on one side of the road, or to an open soybean field on the other side, while maintaining a keen eye on their prized meal.

"Eight, I count eight of them," Alex stated. "Looks like four mature and four immature bald eagles."

Art confirmed Alex's count. "Yes, that's what I see also. That's a lot of eagles at one road kill. Normally, I see one or two. They might have been a group that was starting to migrate south and spotted the kill."

We watched as the group of eagles all stayed within a couple hundred feet of their food.

Curiosity in our group started to get the best of us.

Slowly, we drove up the gravel road to see what they were feeding on. When we were within twenty feet, we got out of the car to make a positive observation of the kill.

"What in the world is that?" I asked, looking at the dead animal about eighteen inches long with dark grayish-brown fur and a small head and mouth."

"I'm not sure, but I know it's not a dog," Deputy Alex North replied.

DNR Agent Art Swenson recognized it. "Looks like a badger. My guess is that a local farmer may have hit it intentionally. You don't want to accidentally discover one of these cornered on your farm."

Looking at the teeth, Art Swenson's statement was an understatement. Even though it had a small mouth about the size of a small dog, on the top and bottom of the mouth were six perfectly lined teeth. However, it was the huge incisors that caught everyone's attention. The four incisors were a half inch longer than the other teeth.

This was a mouth that was designed to tear something apart. Everyone agreed that they would not want to encounter a badger cornered in some farmer's feed bin.

Art told us, "I remember a friend telling me that his dog had cornered one of those on his farm. He heard the dog growling. The next thing he heard was a couple yelps, followed by silence.

Don't ever get too close to a badger."

The eagles had apparently opened the carcass and were feasting on the internal organs and the flesh of the animal. All the ribs were left exposed, and by the color of the remaining flesh, the animal hadn't been dead too long.

"Art, I hate to correct an animal expert," I asserted, "but that's not a road kill. Check out the exposed ribs and legs."

Thanks to the eagles, everything was showing.

"None of them are broken."

Art Swenson looked in a little closer at the bloody mess of an animal. "You're right; I don't see any broken bones. Wonder what killed it?"

"There's a blood trail," Alex broke in, pointing to some spots of blood on the side of the road.

"Well, look at you. Trying to teach our expert how to track a wounded animal?" I teased her.

"I go deer hunting every year," she told me. "I've had to track a wounded deer through the woods for over a half a mile."

"And, I thought you said you were a crack shot?" I joked.

We walked down the road about thirty yards following the faint trail of blood drops.

Art pointed, "There it is."

There was a pool of dried blood next to the road and some fur next to it.

"Looks like someone shot it. I'm surprised someone let it get close enough to shoot. And, with that corn field so close to the road, you would think the badger would have sensed someone and took off into the field, long before they got a chance to shoot," Alex commented.

Art replied, "Well, like I said, farmers don't exactly like these critters in their farms. Probably had his hunting rifle in the pickup and took a lucky shot from a distance."

As they were examining the kill site, Alex spotted something in the road shining in the morning sunlight. It looked like glass scattered on the gravel road. She walked another forty feet to check it out.

I asked her, "What are you looking at?"

"There is some broken glass in the road," she answered.

"Someone probably threw a bottle out the window of their vehicle," Art replied.

"No, this is flat glass – lots of small pieces."

Looking closer at the fragments, she called back to us, "Guys, there's blood on the glass."

Chapter 2

Meetings

The Previous Day

A large group of us had gathered as part of the quarterly meeting of the regional law enforcement task force. This quarter's meeting had been shifted from Minneapolis to Duluth. It was the perfect time of the year to move a meeting to Duluth.

Even in mid-October, the area still brings tourists to the North Shore area along Lake Superior. They come to enjoy the last of the colors of the tamarack, aspen, maple and oak trees, which contrast with the green needles of the other pines, and are made picture perfect by the blue reflections of the big lake.

For our group of seasoned law enforcement agents, the beautiful scenery helped unclutter our minds from our regular jobs. Although the peak of the color was almost over, there were just enough traces to bring a smile of enjoyment as we arrived in town.

Our meeting was scheduled for the Duluth Radisson Hotel's meeting room. It was well attended by many of the local and federal agencies in the area.

There were representatives of the county sheriff's offices – both from Minnesota and Wisconsin, the city police chiefs – from Duluth and Superior, and representatives from the FBI, DEA, ATF, Bureau of Indian Affairs, Department of Justice, U.S. Marshalls, Homeland Security, Coast Guard, Immigration and Border Patrol agents.

Looking like a who's who in law enforcement in the area, by moving the quarterly meeting, it allowed a few of the local agents to participate in the meeting and establish the necessary ties to some of their counterparts in the room. Ever since 9/11, one of our enforcement agency's missions was to improve communications with the other enforcement agencies.

Our meeting was broken into two sessions. In the morning, there was a light meeting. The emphasis was on introducing the agents, and what their major concerns were that might require observation or assistance by the other departments.

Barbs were often heard flying in each of our sessions between the agents. It was an attempt to lighten the atmosphere, while dealing with serious concepts of learning proper communication protocols between the agencies.

By afternoon, the discussions took on a more serious level. There were new reporting criteria; release of information requirements and a few other new federal communication mandates that were to be handed down to the various enforcement agencies.

After our meetings, the group met for dinner in the 360-degree rotating dining room at the top of the hotel. Taking up almost half the tables of the restaurant, we had an early dinner, which was timed perfectly to allow us to enjoy the view at sunset.

The tables were arranged leaving a few tables between the regular customers and the law enforcement group. This gave us the separation that allowed us to talk freely with each other and not disturb the other customers.

As the representative agent for the FBI, I sat at a table with Agent Jackson Smith from the DEA, Agent Art Swenson from the Wisconsin DNR, and Deputy Alex North from the Lake County Sheriff's Department. Deputy North was filling in for her Sheriff who was busy on another assignment. It gave her a chance to meet the heads of the departments.

While we were enjoying the view overlooking the Duluth harbor, our discussions led to our individual backgrounds, and how each one of us got into law enforcement.

We all came from slightly different backgrounds. However, the common point we shared was the fact that we got into law enforcement because we wanted to make a difference and protect the way things were when we were younger.

This was exactly what these meetings were designed for. It was a time to get to know the personal side of the other agents as well as understand what responsibilities they had in their own departments.

Contacts are essential in today's law enforcement.

While we were eating, I chuckled when Alex North mentioned that she was hired when the department confused her name for a man's name.

Somehow, after talking to her earlier at our meetings, I had the impression that she had definitely earned her way into her job, once the department realized she was female. Even with long brown hair and a good athletic physique, she had an air about her that told someone that she wouldn't put up with too much guff.

Although, after being at the table with us, she was starting to relax with the table talk. I was starting to see that there was a personal side that she kept hidden.

Art Swenson informed us that he always enjoyed hunting and fishing. He was looking for a job that would actually pay him for finding the hidden hot spots other people had located.

That brought a round of smiles from the group.

After enjoying a great steak dinner and the discussions, which flowed across the table, Art asked those at our table if anyone wanted to join him in some pheasant hunting in the morning. It was supposed to be one of those exceptional Saturday mornings for this part of the country – sunny, temperatures in the 60's and a light south wind.

I thought about it for a moment. "You know, I'd love to, but I didn't bring any clothes for that type of outdoor event. Even though this is a casual meeting, and I wore jeans, that's as far as my field clothes go for this trip."

"So, Mark, there's a Target and Walmart in town," Art quipped. "Run yourself out and pick up a pair of cheap hiking boots and a sweatshirt. You already have the jeans. I'm sure I can find you an orange safety vest to wear, so that the rest of us can locate where you are, and put you in our sights. How about you Alex?"

"I haven't been out pheasant hunting in years. Sure, I'd love to."

Jackson Smith was the only one at the table that had to beg out of the invite. Unfortunately, he had to travel to North Dakota

Sunday night and his family wanted to spend some time with him before he headed out of town.

This was a common problem with all the members of the group, and we understood it very well.

"Okay," I told the group. "You bent my arm. You suppose they sell Wisconsin licenses at Walmart? Plus, you got enough firepower?"

"I think I can manage it," Art Swenson told me. "I have a shotgun in the car and a couple at home. I think I can find one with a slightly bent barrel just special for you. How about an early breakfast around seven? We can get there by nine or so. Can you handle a 12 gauge, or would you rather use your service revolver?"

He was definitely trying to get my goat. I laughed. "I'd rather have several pellets in the air at that range, rather than just one if you don't mind. Besides, as a FBI agent, I'm only allowed to carry my one bullet in my shirt pocket."

So, it was agreed. Alex and I made a quick stop at the store for the appropriate license, and in my case, a good pair of boots.

Alex carried a pair in her car.

Back to the Hunt

As we were examining the badger's kill site, Alex had spotted something in the road shining in the morning sunlight. It looked like glass on the gravel road. She walked another forty feet to check it out.

"What are you looking at?" I asked.

"There's some broken glass in the road," she answered.

"Someone probably just threw a bottle out of their vehicle," Art replied.

"No, this is flat glass – lots of small pieces." As she looked closer, she called back to us. "There's dried blood on the glass."

We walked over to check it out.

Sure enough, there were spots of blood on many of the pieces of glass.

Where did it come from and how did it get there?

As we were checking out the glass, which was scattered only on one side of the road, I happened to glance down the road. About a hundred yards down the road, it looked as though some of the weeds had been disturbed in a small area.

"Let's move to the center of the road," I told the others. "There might be a reason for all of this, and until we know for sure, we don't want to disturb things." I pointed to the weeds down the road.

"Art, how'd you like to stay near the car and make sure no-one drives down the road until we check this out. Alex, let's take a walk down the road."

We walked down the gravel road a hundred yards. There we found evidence of a set of tracks from a vehicle that had driven off the road into the edge of the marsh. You could hardly see it for all the tall weeds and cattails near the road. It was the same tall weeds that left us the clue that something had departed the road. Had the weeds not been bent over, you would have missed everything.

You couldn't see very much from the road. I decided to venture into the brush a little ways to check it out.

"Dang, every time I get a new set of boots, it seems that someone wants to ruin them for me," I told Alex, as I stepped from the gravel road into the marshy weeds.

It was definitely soft ground. My boots quickly found a wet spot and started to fill with water as my footsteps sunk down into the marsh.

Alex shouted out to me, "Mark, careful that you don't hit a muskrat run in that marsh. Before you know it, you'll be up to your waist in water."

It was a good reminder. Muskrats make runs under the weeds leading to their dens under the shoreline. If you step in one, before you know it, you're waist deep in the water. I thanked her for reminding me.

The vehicle did not get very far with the soft dirt. It was only thirty feet from the spot it left the road. It must have been traveling at a very fast rate of speed to get that far in the soft muck.

As I approached the car, I could see the driver's window was open or missing.

Getting closer, my suspicions were confirmed – the driver was dead. He had been shot in the neck.

"Alex, you better shout down the road to Agent Swenson.
"Tell him to call the local Sheriff. We have a body."

Chapter 3

Evidence

The next hour brought a number of squad cars rushing to the quiet, gravel road. It only took about ten minutes before the first of the Sheriff's cars arrived.

Agent Art Swenson had backed his car about two hundred feet down the road, and used it to block off any traffic from the north.

Alex North had walked about the same distance to the south and made sure any local traffic from that direction would not disturb the scene until the local Sheriff's deputies arrived.

We were hoping to preserve any evidence that might still exist at the scene.

The question was; what happened here, and why? Looking at the circumstances, we figured our hunting trip was coming to an end.

When the first of the Sheriff's deputies arrived, I introduced myself as FBI Special Agent Mark Lawson; and showed him where the vehicle came to rest in the marsh. It was a dark grey Toyota Camry. Actually, it was a very dirty Camry, covered with clumps of weeds and dirt, caked all over the car.

If you were looking for a missing vehicle from the air, you might have missed it with all the debris on the car covering almost every shiny part of the body.

Looking closer, there was a single bullet hole low in the corner of the passenger's side of the windshield. The driver's window had been blown out.

In-between, the driver, a male about thirty years old, dressed in casual clothing laid slumped over in the bloody seat. A bullet hole was evident, which appeared to have gone through his neck.

"What do you make of it?" the deputy asked me.

"Glass on the road indicates he was shot as he drove down the gravel road. I'm not sure if he was conscious or not before he ran off the road and ended up here in the marsh," I told him. "He was probably losing blood quickly if an artery was severed by the impact."

"Could have been an accidental shooting. Someone hunting squirrels perhaps," the deputy mentioned.

"Not likely," I stated. "Someone killed a badger a few yards further up the road. I'm guessing it might have been the same person.

"I might be wrong, but my gut tells me someone was waiting for whoever this is. The badger just showed up in the wrong place at the wrong time. Anyone in the area, who might have heard the shots, probably thought someone was hunting in the area."

"You would have thought the badger would have smelled someone in the area and headed off into the field," the deputy told me.

"That's what we thought as well. You need to establish where the shooter was. In addition, you might want to check for rabies. It might have looked threatening to someone hiding in the trees along the road, wondering whether it had rabies or not. They probably shot it to eliminate it," I suggested to him. "You might ask DNR Agent Art Swenson, down the road, to help you on that. He could tell you if badgers get rabies or not."

"Too bad the bullet hit his neck and not something solid. It will be hard to find it in the corn field," the deputy suggested.

"Well, you might have gotten lucky. If it was the same shooter, we know where the badger was when it was shot. Like the dead man, the bullet didn't hit any bones. I'd be willing to bet the bullet is buried in the dirt right behind the pool of blood left by the badger."

While the deputy and I walked back to check out the kill spot of the badger, other deputies had arrived and were starting to search the road and woods for clues.

As we walked, I could hear a sloshing sound coming from my new boots. When I purchased them, it said they were waterproof. Unfortunately, right now, that meant the water that seeped over the top of my boots was not going to be running out of them any time soon.

Inspecting the site where the animal was shot, I pointed out the tufts of fur that were blown out of the body of the badger.

"It is hard to say exactly where the badger was hit, but I'm sure the experts can match the fur color with the body to tell us. If the fur is any indication, the bullet should be somewhere in the couple-foot region between the corpse and the slope of the ditch behind the badger."

As we looked carefully, I spotted an area that looked like an anthill.

"I'll bet you could find a slug a few inches into the soil beneath that spot," I told him. "That looks like a rebound splatter from the impact of the slug."

The deputy had his photographer take some pictures of the area. Then, he borrowed a hunting knife to probe the soil.

About three inches into the dirt, his probe hit something hard. We got lucky, it was the slug.

As he removed the slug from the ground, he turned to me and said, ".38 slug. That means a handgun, not a rifle. He was close when he shot the car. That's assuming we are looking at the same shooter. You need to be a good shot to hit a moving car. It would have been much easier to hit it from a distance with a rifle and scope."

With the assumption of a high accuracy range of about fifty feet or less for a handgun, the deputies started checking the trees for signs of footprints.

Their hunch was right-on. Behind one large oak tree, one of the deputies found disturbed soil from someone who shuffled their feet. That must have been the shooters location. The deputies were definitely making progress.

The search of the road for footprints or car tracks was difficult. Since the shooting happened, it was difficult to determine if the tracks in the road were from the shooter, or simply from local farmers just driving down the road.

We didn't think it had rained for at least two days, so the tracks should be recent.

The deputies were going to try and get tread prints from each of the local farmers, and anyone else who drove down the road the rest of the day. They were hoping to be able to eliminate as many of the tracks on the road as possible.

However, part of that answer would relate to the coroner's results. They would have to determine the actual time of death.

Presumably, the badger died shortly before the person drove into the shooters sights. With an accurate time of death, it might determine if they could use any of the tire tracks.

For Alex North, Art Swenson and myself, it was time to let the local Sheriff's department handle their case. There was very little else we could do, except for getting in the way.

I told the deputy that I would touch base in a couple days to see if they found any information on the case. Then, the three of us decided it was time to call it a day.

With all that police traffic, all the pheasants would have been chased away, anyway.

Driving back to the Twin Cities, I was grateful I still had dry shoes back in my car along with my dirty socks from yesterday. It would have been a long ride to the cities if I had to wear my wet boots or go barefoot.

I did think it was odd that the shooter hadn't used a shotgun or rifle. Especially, since it was hunting season. This time of year, someone seen with a long gun would have blended in perfectly with all the hunters.

Chapter 4

The Rookie

Two Harbors, MN

It was a sunny day as the iron ore carrier Calvin Wroth entered port, in Two Harbors, Minnesota. It was a scheduled stop for the vessel. From there, it would be hauling 43,900 tons of iron ore pellets from Two Harbors to Sault Ste. Marie, Canada.

After the ship was loaded, the passage across the big lake would take about twenty hours to cover the 371 nautical miles (426 statute miles). It was almost the entire east/west length of Lake Superior. With another four hours to unload the cargo, barring any delays, the ship would be back in Two Harbors in two days.

She was on the second of a four-trip assignment. After that, they would get new orders stating which port they were shipping from, what their cargo would be, and where the cargo needed to be delivered.

The Calvin Wroth was equipped with an auto-unloader. A conveyor was located under the holds and brought the cargo to an outlet chute at the back of the ship. Unfortunately, to use this feature, which cut unloading times drastically and improved the profitability of the ship, you had to have a terminal that could pick up the cargo at the end of the ship terminal using another conveyor. Only a few ports on the Great Lakes had a facility designed to handle the Calvin Wroth (as the planned designs for off-loading newer ships were changed after the Calvin Wroth's construction).

By mid-October, the rush was on to haul as much cargo as possible before the weather made the big lake impossible to navigate. Lake Superior is known for its late season storms, which can unexpectedly bring high waves and icy conditions. The lake is a place that mariners have feared come November. Ever since the sinking of the giant ore ship Edmond Fitzgerald, the Gales of November have been on the minds of the shipping crews.

As the ship was being loaded at the ore dock, several members of the crew left the ship on their normal crew rotation. Their two-month shift on the long ore boat was over, and four new crewmembers were waiting at the dock to replace the crew after taking their month off.

One of the replacement crewmembers was Stubby O'Shea. Unlike the others, he was new to the Calvin Wroth. The others were coming back from their scheduled extended shore leave.

Stubby had been a longshoreman in New Jersey for fifteen years. After working the docks for all those years, he decided that he wanted to try working "on" the ships, instead of loading and unloading their contents.

All of the ships Stubby loaded or unloaded in his old job were salties – ships that went across the ocean. For his first "on ship" experience, he decided he wanted to try working on a "laker."

A laker was a ship that stayed in the Great Lakes. Because of the limitations at the locks on the St. Lawrence Seaway, the lakers tended to be slightly smaller than many of the salties, and they ran trips of shorter durations. However, just as there seems to be exceptions to everything, every once in a while there are smaller salties that make the occasional runs into the Great Lakes.

The larger lakers, those that approached 1019 feet or less could still operate in Lake Superior, Lake Michigan, Lake Erie, and Huron. The locks at Sault Ste. Marie allowed the larger ships to pass, while the older locks entering the St. Lawrence Seaway restricted the size of the vessel.

These larger vessels were primarily bulk carriers that carried rock, ore, grain, limestone, cement, gypsum or coal. From Lake Superior, they hauled their cargos from ports with the names the likes of Two Harbors, Silver Bay, Thunder Bay, Duluth and Superior east to ports both along the lake and off into the other Great Lakes.

Stubby was short in stature. Built like a fireplug. He had gotten the appropriate nickname years ago from other longshoremen who watched him lay worker after worker on the pavement. For those that really ticked him off, a wrap over the head might get them in line after they tried to harass him about his short stature.

It didn't take long for his reputation to spread on the wharf. This was one tough longshoreman, and anyone that didn't think Stubby could hold his own, was about to find out the hard way – with a sudden dip in the cold water.

Stubby looked over the huge ship. He had signed on as an Ordinary Seaman. It was a fancy name for a deck hand and helper.

At a starting pay of $55,000, for what amounted to six-months work, it would be his job to assist a licensed Able Seaman on the boat for the shipping season, handling the ropes, latching the holds, and making sure everything topside was secured before they shoved off.

After his initial training period, he could take the test for the licensed Able Seaman's certificate. With the Coast Guard certificate came a boost in rank as well as a bump in pay.

As soon as he was on-board, he threw his sea bag in his quarters and reported for duty. With only four hours needed to load the ore at the dock, learning the ship would have to be his first priority.

Stubby's training was fast and firm. Learning where not to be was most important. Work on ships is definitely dangerous if you don't pay attention. Things move and the last thing they wanted was a new man that was constantly in the wrong place, where he might get injured.

Another crewmember was assigned the task of training him on this first cruise. After that, he was on his own to follow one of the Able Seaman's directions at each port.

"Just follow me," Swede, the tall, lanky, grey haired crewmember, who carried the title of a licensed Able Seaman, told him. "Don't do anything, unless I tell you."

Stubby had no intentions of it. He knew from his days as a longshoreman that people that didn't listen, tended to lose fingers or hands when things unexpectedly moved.

"What happened to the man I replaced?" Stubby politely asked. "He retire?"

"Nah! Superstitious runt. We hung a raven from above his bunk one night. Next port, he was gone."

Stubby didn't need to ask any more questions. He knew the ways of the longshoremen. In Jersey, if someone was weird, they would pressure them to quit, or occasionally, if needed, they would make sure they simply disappeared, never to be seen again. It was the way things were done. He assumed things on the ships were handled in the same manor.

The ship was loading right on schedule. The trick for loading the ore was to load it progressively from one end to the other by conveyor.

The ship was slowly settling down in the water from the weight of the ore. As the final holds were loaded, the crews started using the crane to move the covers over the holds, which kept the water out the ship when she was underway. The holds could be secured once they were out of the harbor, and the ship cleared the breakwater.

So far, the forecast looked good for sailing to Sault Ste. Marie. A five to ten mph wind from the south was almost perfect.

At 858 feet long by 105 feet wide, the Calvin Wroth was not the longest or shortest of the ore carriers. Fully loaded, it would draft 41 feet of water. However, with low water at the end of summer, it could only be filled to the 21 feet 11 inch draft line to prevent problems at the harbors.

Built around 1970, it was an older style ore ship with the helm in the front of the ship. The Great Lakes Fleet Inc. owned a fleet of ore carriers, which operated on the Great Lakes, and the Calvin Wroth was part of their fleet.

As the ship's horn sounded one long blast, Swede told Stubby, "Time to stow the lines."

Stubby had been on the other end of this task many times in New Jersey. He followed Swede to his station in the stern where they operated the winch that retrieved the heavy ropes that held the ship firmly to the dock. As the last line came in, he could hear the engines coming to life – the thrusters were cranking up to nudge the ship away from the dock.

Stubby watched as the vessel slowly moved back. The water was churning like a whirlpool in a river, between the ship and dock. There were thrusters in the bow and stern of the ship.

From a small stack, black smoke billowed from the bow as a generator provided the electricity for the front thrusters.

Soon, he would hear the three short blasts of the horn (indicating to anyone in the harbor that the ship was leaving the terminal). Then, the twin stern-stacks would change from light smoke to billowing large amounts of black smoke, as the main diesel engines were engaged to pull the heavily loaded ship back from the loading dock.

The stern was about forty feet from the dock when Stubby noticed something strange. As he scanned down the length of the ship from his location at the back, he noticed the bow was only ten feet from the dock. Slowly, it was catching up.

However, that wasn't the problem. The ship seemed to bend in the middle. The back half of the ship was at an even forty feet.

"What the?" Stubby said.

Before he got another word out, Swede answered. "That's what spooked your predecessor. This ship bends in the middle. Just watch. As we back up, the hull will straighten. You'll see."

Stubby watched as they started to move back. Sure enough, even with a full load of ore, the ship straightened out, like an arrow, as the main engines strained to pull the ship back.

"Do all ships do that?" Stubby asked. "I don't remember seeing that on other ships."

"Nope! Just this one," came the answer.

After the ship cleared the breakwater, and all the hold covers were secured, Swede and Stubby went below for dinner. Their shift was almost over. Before they ate, Swede gave Stubby the required short lesson in lifeboat training.

As they headed for the mess hall for food, Stubby asked Swede, "Any other strange things I need to know?"

"Well, the ship has had a few problems in its days. Earlier this year, we ran aground. We got a new skipper after that one.

"When the ship was new, before she had carried a single load, the engine room had a fire. Couple of guys in a lower level died from asphyxiation. It took a year to repair the vessel.

"It had a few other problems. In 1973, it struck the stern of another vessel when working in ice off Mackinac. She was reconditioned from 1981-1987. I'm not sure what was done. Rumor has it they considered mothballing her along with the older boats.

"She had two more collisions – in 1994 with a ship, and in 2000 with a dock. The one in 2000 reportedly damaged the side plates. Then, there was 2006. We lost our rudder and it took three days before one of our sister ships got us in tow.

Talk about bobbing around in the lake. Good thing we didn't hit a storm.

"You know about the bend. I was told the ship was built in two sections – a little over 400 feet each. Then, they welded them together. The ship was designed to flex to take stress off the point where the sections were welded together. I'm not sure they expected that much flex.

"Your predecessor thought they didn't repair the side plates properly. He figured one day, in a good fall gale, the ship would disappear. He wanted off in the worst way, before the November Gales."

"Swede, stop scaring the rookie," Stubby heard the cook threaten Swede from behind the counter, waving a chopping knife.

Stubby was starting to realize why a superstitious crewman might want to get off the ship. With a ship that had that much history, including a bend in the middle, it was amazing the entire crew didn't want to jump ship.

The outbound passage to Sault Ste. Marie went on without a hitch. Stubby watched to see if any other members of the crew wanted to play any games on a rookie. It was a small crew of only twenty-five people.

Somehow, he expected the worst. At least for this first passage, they laid off.

It would take Stubby a while to get used to the crew shifts. Generally, they had four hours on and eight hours off. That was with the exception of when anything urgent came up. Then, they were all expected to show up when needed. With short trips, it didn't leave long periods of down time.

The passage from Two Harbors to the Sault Ste. Marie was smooth. The light wind that was blowing from the south, gave the illusion of standing waves on the horizon.

The boat was out far enough on the lake that occasionally you could just make out one shoreline. From the deck, it was as though the waves were lapping at the sky. The only sounds were the droning of the huge engines. It was a sound that most seasoned seamen learned to ignore. That was until something changed. Then, they sensed something was wrong.

When the ship pulled into the dock in Sault Ste. Marie, Stubby watched from his station on the stern line, while assisting Swede. The ship was gently pushing itself into the dock by use of the thrusters.

Sure enough, there it was. There was a definite bend in the middle of the ship, as the thrusters unevenly pushed the long vessel from both ends toward the loading dock.

Once the ship was tied up, it was a massive job for the entire deck crew to assist in unloading the ship, along with bringing any supplies and fuel onboard. On top of that, there was cleaning or painting that would be on his list, before getting the ship ready for the return trip.

Stubby was starting to wonder if a job onboard a salty would have been easier. At least there would have been a few more days between ports.

Chapter 5

Storm Warnings

When the Calvin Wroth pushed off from the loading dock at Sault Ste. Marie, word came down to the crew – make sure the hatches are fastened down firmly. Captain Taccetta had informed the crew that they were expecting some turbulent weather as they headed back down the big lake.

As a result, Stubby and Swede rechecked the deck once all the holds were capped. Nothing was left to shift should they hit some inclement weather.

Swede had done this routine many times in the past fifteen years. He had seen how the big lake could change from a light chop to huge waves in just a matter of hours.

As they reached the steps leading from the deck down to the crew's quarters, another crewman – Blackie, bumped into Stubby's shoulder on the narrow steps.

"Well, you must be the greenhorn. I heard we had a hawsepiper that joined us in Two Harbors. You better hold Swede's hand up there. We don't go back for swimmers."

"Hawsepiper" was the term given to seamen that attempted to come up through the ranks rather than going to one of the union training academies. The term hawsepiper comes from the tube through which an anchor chain is drawn into a boat.

Swede turned to Stubby, "Don't mind Blackie. He works in the engine room. It's hot down there and I think he's hit his head too many times on low hanging pipes. He's always that way with all the new crewmembers. Just ignore him."

"Where did he get the name Blackie?" Stubby asked, looking at a man who had such pale skin that it looked as though he had never been out in the sun.

"First cruise. He had to clean out one of the main shaft's bearings down there. He came out so black with grease, the name stuck.

"You get seasick?" Swede asked Stubby.

"Don't know. How bad is it going to get?"

"Depends! We'll have to see if we are going into the waves or if they are coming from the side. I've seen waves splash right over the bow. You wouldn't think the lake could get as rough as the ocean, but for some reason it can. I'm sure they're floodin the inner hull as we speak to lower the center of gravity."

Stubby thought about it for a few minutes. He was used to seeing the ships riding high after the cargo was unloaded. Sometimes, it was a thirty to forty foot difference in how the ship sat in the water. When the ship was empty, to keep it stable in the water, they would pump water into the lower hull to add weight. Then, when they were nearing the port for loading their cargo, they would begin pumping it out to increase the carrying capacity of the ship.

He wondered how much water the lower hull could hold. Would it really make the ship ride deeper in the water? From his position up on the ship, he couldn't see the markings on the hull indicating the draft of the ship. (The draft markings assisted the Captain in knowing how deep in the water the ship rode to prevent it from hitting bottom.)

"Word to the wise," Swede leaned over and told him. "You might want to skip dinner tonight. If it gets real rough tonight, you'll be glad you did."

Stubby was a tough guy. He feared no one. On the other hand, he had not experienced really rough weather for any length of time. Mentally, he told himself that he could handle anything. What he couldn't guarantee was what his stomach might do.

This would be a good test. He would take Swede's advice and tough it out. As a precaution, he had picked up some motion sickness pills at a pharmacy, just before boarding the ship the first day. He had stashed them in his sea bag. Stubby decided it might be a good time to take one before hitting the sack tonight.

By dinnertime, Lake Superior was starting to get choppy. The big ship plowed through the six to eight foot waves with only a slight rock from side to side. Stubby was starting to wonder if he really needed to skip dinner.

As he walked one of the inner halls heading towards the mess hall, he stopped to read a posting by the 2nd Mate Joe Labonta. It was the weather warning Swede had mentioned earlier.

The forecast was for thunderstorms with high winds and rain. Winds were expected to pick up to forty miles-per-hour with seas of up to fifteen feet expected.

Okay, that would be a little rougher than what they were currently experiencing. However, the bow sat some fifty feet above the waterline. A ship the size of a city block should be able to handle it without a problem.

As he was considering his options, one of the cook's helpers, Eric, walked by.

"Have you been in rough seas before?" he inquired. "If you're not sure how your gut will handle it, I wouldn't eat much. It's no fun cleaning up the deck when the ship is pitching, and there are no maids on this ship to go around behind you."

"Is it really going to get that rough?" Stubby asked.

"It can. It's not the regular waves. What happens is that they come from different directions. When they merge, a fifteen-foot wave can end up as a twenty-five footer. Since we are empty, this rusty bucket of bolts will be bobbing like a cork in a moving bucket. When you start to hear the rivets creek and groan, then you know it's getting rough. Besides, you may get the call to go up on deck if anything starts to come loose. That's your job, not mine. I just sit down here watching the rookies turn green."

Stubby decided he could skip one meal. It wouldn't hurt his diet. He had put on five pounds in the past week with the lack of heavy lifting he was used to on the docks. In the past, all that activity had kept him in top shape. Now, with the downtime on the ship, he would have to work out in the crew's quarters to stay in shape.

As Stubby was finishing his conversation with Eric, he felt a large hand on his shoulder. It was Swede.

"Let's go up on deck," he told him. "Time for one more check, before it gets rough. I'd rather spot a loose chain now, than when it is raining in another hour."

It was a good idea. The two of them made a check of all the holds and the chained up equipment on the deck. As they did, you could feel the wind picking up. The storm was still miles away, but the wind and waves were already announcing its presence. It felt strange. Stubby could see the lightning in the distance, but the thunder, carried by the water, was just a muffled groan.

"That storm's still twenty miles away," Swede pointed out, as he showed Stubby how to attach his safety line to the railings when up on deck. When things got a little rougher, it would be required of anyone working up there. The last thing the crew wanted was for a crewmember to be swept off the deck. "Remember, Lake Superior's water stays around thirty-nine degrees. You don't last long at that temperature."

It took over an hour to walk the ship and check all the equipment. By the time they got back inside, the waves were up to nine feet. Walking the halls, the two men looked as though they had been drinking. They gently staggered back to the crew's quarters, occasionally using the walls to keep their balance.

Around nine bells, the rain hit. Most of the experienced crew didn't seem to be bothered by the rolling of the ship. They had been through it many times before.

So far, Stubby was handling it okay. Except for the lightning, the storm wasn't that bad.

When the lightning bolted through the sky, it was as though the whole sky lit up. Then, the thunder cracked outside as if there was a full set of cannons on a warship just off their sides. The sound penetrated through the steel hull and echoed through the empty holds as if they were designed to be huge bass speakers. They reverberated with each lightning bolt.

Stubby was enjoying the light and sound effects of the storm. It was very different from what he was used to seeing and hearing from a storm on shore.

He settled back into his bunk, letting the ship rock him to sleep. Twice, he woke up with the loud sound of something in the ship falling off a shelf. Each time he quickly dozed back off. The sedative effect in the seasick pills was working and helped him drift off into dreamland.

In the early morning, when Stubby woke up, the ship appeared to be much more stable than it was during the night. The storm was gone and the sun would soon be shining through the porthole. Fortunately, there had not been any problems up on the deck last night that needed attention.

With the exception of a dry mouth from the seasick pills, Stubby was pleased that he had weathered the storm without problems. Now, he was hungry. His lack of dinner last night was gnawing at him. He would have just enough time for a quick breakfast before having to hit the deck.

"Well, green horn, you look okay after a night's sleep."

It was the cook's helper, Eric, whom Stubby had talked to last night.

"Slept like a baby," Stubby told him. "How rough did it get last night."

"Oh, it was just a light blow. We get them every couple of weeks. Hopefully, you'll get used to them before we hit a big storm. When your buddy Swede doesn't eat for a couple days, then you'll know you hit a real storm."

Stubby ate a full breakfast before heading back up on deck for the arrival back in Two Harbors.

The covers on the holds needed to be unlatched and removed before the ship reached the terminal. There was a mountain of ore pellets on shore awaiting their arrival.

Chapter 6

Follow Up

FBI Agent Mark Lawson

After being out of town, I was swamped with paperwork, so I waited a couple of days before contacting the Douglas County Sheriff's Office. I was hoping that some of the lab results were back before checking to see if they were making progress.

The Sheriff was not in when I tried to contact him the first time. About an hour later, I received a return call.

"Mark, this is Rick Bernaski, Douglas County Sheriff, I had a note that you tried calling earlier."

"Thanks Rick, I wasn't planning on calling you so soon after our meeting in Duluth, last Friday. I suppose you heard that three of us found a body in your territory, on Saturday, while we were pheasant hunting.

"I was just calling to see if you had any updates on the case, I told your deputy I would check back in a couple days."

"So, which one of you couldn't tell the difference between a pheasant and a Toyota?" he asked. "I asked my deputy if he checked to see if your guns had been fired."

"Thanks! I think we were all using 12 gauge shotguns. Have you ID'd the victim? Someone was a great shot to hit a moving car like that, especially, at close range."

"Yeah. That's what I thought when we reviewed the case. I need to give you credit for locating that slug we dug out of the dirt. With the soft dirt, the striations on the bullet, caused by the gun's barrel, were still on the slug.

"Turns out we were able to match the gun used to another killing six months ago, which is still an open case that we are still working on.

"We did have one surprise. The name on the victim's driver's license and fingerprints didn't match. Fingerprints matched an old robbery case in New Jersey. Says that his name was Bo Callahan. Nothing on him since, except that records indicated that he still lives in New Jersey."

"So, what was our dead man doing on a lonely dirt road in Wisconsin?" I inquired.

"We checked the area farmers. One told us he remembered seeing someone in the area with a camera. They didn't think anything of it at the time and didn't remember what the person looked like.

"My guess is that is why the shooter wasn't carrying a shotgun. Who would remember someone with a camera in an area with lots of wildlife?"

"Sounds like you have it under control. Let me know if you need anything," I told him.

"Well, there is one thing. Can you run a more detailed check on the dead guy? Maybe one of your people could gather up some additional details on him. I'm a little surprised we couldn't find a lot more. No wife, kids, not even relatives."

"Yeah, that is odd. I'll see what we can find," I told Sheriff Bernaski.

"Oh, another thing," Sheriff Bernaski told me, "the next time you want to go pheasant hunting in my county, let me know. I'll have someone release a few birds so you can at least get off one shot."

"And I thought that meeting was to develop friendly contacts," I suggested. "I'll let you know what we find."

I had a feeling from the start that I would end up involved in the investigation. The thought of someone using a handgun for an assassination sounded too professional for northern Wisconsin. It appeared to be a set-up for the deceased.

Definitely not a random shooting.

I had a note from Alex North, asking if I had heard any additional information about the man we discovered shot in his car in the marsh, so, I gave her a call to let her know what I had been told.

She told me how she enjoyed our outing, well, that is until we ran into the shooting. After talking for a while, she told me I could join them deer hunting if I wanted to finish breaking in my new boots.

I told her that it would take that long for them to dry out. Thanking her for the offer, I got back to my job – attempting to reduce the pile of papers on my desk.

I was working on several cases at the same time. Unfortunately, that was the nature of the job. My job was to coordinate the regional efforts on each of the cases.

So far, in the past two months, we were working on two bank robberies, a possible embezzlement case at a financial institution, assisting on three murder cases that appeared to involve felons that had been released in the past couple years, and then there were the other cases that required minor work that was going on long-term in an attempt to solve them.

The request by Douglas County Sheriff, Rick Bernaski, was just one more piece of paper on top of the mountain. One by one the progress of our group rotated cases from the top of the pile to the bottom and then hopefully to the solved pile.

I wondered how the agents used to handle all the files before computers. If everything had to be done using a paper copy, the small stack on my desk would have been pile that qualified to be named an official mountain in Minnesota.

I caught up on the current status of all my agent's cases and followed up with phone calls to several of them, making sure we were all working on the same page, before heading off to my next meeting.

Oh, yes, I did make contact with my counterparts in New Jersey on the Douglas County case. They told me they would look into it and get back to me as soon as they had some information.

For now, I had a community meeting in Minneapolis that required me to make an appearance.

Just one more part of the job.

Chapter 7

Port

After his second trip to the Canadian port of Sault Ste. Marie, Stubby was starting to get a handle on his duties.

Stubby O'Shea on the Calvin Wroth

The officers tended to stay separate from the working class, but one by one, I was starting to know everyone.

Before the ship made port back in Two Harbors, we had a discussion in the mess room. A few of us needed some supplies, and the ship had a policy that when anyone went ashore, they took with them the list from other members of the crew that were still required to be onboard, to stay and work.

In my case, it was items that I had not packed the first time, before I boarded the ship, plus a few items I had used up.

As a result, it was decided that Blackie, myself, and one of the officers – Leo Brasso, our 3rd Mate, would pick up the lists made by our other crewmembers, and find the supplies needed from town.

It took me a while to realize the significance of the three of us going ashore. We represented three of the four groups on the ship – officers, deckhands, and engineering. Only the cooks were not represented, and it appeared that since they knew everyone, they simply gave their list to one of those that were heading off the ship.

Also, we were the crewmembers at the low end of the job seniority in each of our departments. My guess was that Captain Taccetta probably never had to go into town to get the supplies for his group.

Once the ship was docked, and the loading commenced, we climbed down the gangway onto the ore dock, and had one of the shore crew give us a lift to town. Apparently, it was one of the things that was expected by the shipping companies. A person was always available to pick up the crew and take them wherever they needed to go.

Two Harbors was a small town, so there weren't very many stores to choose from. However, for small items like toothpaste, deodorant, etc., one good store would do it. Fortunately, there was a Shopko and a Super One Foods right next to each other. For what we needed, we didn't have to go any further.

It did not take long for us to scratch them off our list of supplies needed.

When we left the store, our transportation was waiting to take us back to the ore dock. Even though the excursion only took just over an hour, it felt good to feel solid ground back under my feet.

Well, almost. I couldn't believe how it felt. Every once in a while, it was as though the ground was moving. This was my first experience of sea legs. Unfortunately, we would not be on shore long enough to convince our minds that we were no longer rocking on a ship.

As the car took us back to the harbor, we saw the exhibit of the old train engines that had been used in the past, to haul ore from the mines to the loading docks. One engine was huge. It was twice as long as many of the other steam engines I had ever seen in the past.

The sign said it was 128 feet long. The Yellowstone Mallet #229 was built in 1943 to haul ore needed for World War II. The huge locomotives stayed in service until 1960. The monster engines would have a working ability of pulling a million pounds per train.

As I looked at the engine, I wondered how much noise it would have made when pulling a string of heavy ore cars a mile long. With its 26 tons of coal and 25,000 gallons of water loaded in the tender, you could have probably heard those behemoths miles down the track.

"That's one of the largest steam engines they ever made," Blackie informed me. "How'd you like the job of shoveling the coal into that one?"

He was right. It might have taken a team of people. However, my guess was that by the time they manufactured the engine, people didn't have to shovel coal anymore. Automated hoppers were probably used. Either way, this was one massive piece of engineering.

As I looked at it, I wondered how the engine on our ship compared. My guess was that the ship had more power. However, these locomotives had to be able to pull those cars up and down the hills to the harbors. That required a great deal of sustained enormous power. Different designs for different jobs.

When we arrived at the massive steel loading dock, we got out of the car. After thanking our driver, with bags of supplies in our arms, we hiked down the ramp to the dock and the loading stairs to the Calvin Wroth.

There was a narrow walkway from the shoreline to the dock. It was a shortcut, so we didn't have to go to the road that led onto the dock. The maintenance road that led to the dock was closed whenever a ship was at the dock and loading was in progress. Leo Brasso took the lead, with Blackie following close behind me. They towered over me as the three of us marched along in a single line.

As we were almost on the loading dock, I thought I heard someone shout, "**Look out!**"

Blackie grabbed me by the arm and yanked me back so severely; I almost fell flat on my back.

"What the?" I declared, before realizing what had just happened.

Leo wasn't as lucky.

Someone was working high above us doing maintenance on the ore dock. They had a bucket of bolts and nuts tied on a rope that they would pull up to the level they were working on. Somehow, it had slipped off the beam it was sitting on, and fallen the nearly fifty feet to the dock.

Since the bucket had been attached to a rope, the bucket swung instead of simply dropping to the level where another dockworker was filling the bucket with the necessary tools needed by the person working on the conveyor system, high above us.

I'm still not sure how, but somehow, Blackie had heard the shout, "Look out!" above the loud roar of the ore conveyor filling our ship. When he spotted the bucket, he grabbed my arm, throwing me off balance and almost into the water.

Leo wasn't as lucky. As the bucket swung on the long rope, like a pendulum, it hit him squarely on the side of the head, knocking him into the water next to the ore dock. I figured that he never even had a chance to see it coming.

Within a minute, sirens were going off on the dock as the emergency shutdown button was engaged.

A few moments later, four members of the shore crew were at the scene helping us get Leo out of the water. Others were coming from the offices on shore as well as people from our ship.

Leo laid out limp in the water. The crystal-clear water of Lake Superior was slowly turning red. It was obvious to everyone that Leo was in serious peril. He was not moving.

One of the dockworkers had quickly jumped into the water and was trying to hand Leo to those on the dock. We stood there, still in shock from the whole event, and it took a moment to realize what had actually happened.

When we attempted to reach out to grab Leo from the water, we could see the damage to the side of Leo's head. He had taken the entire blow right in front of his left ear. His face was a mess.

It only took another minute for help to start to arrive. We weren't sure if he was alive or not by the time the emergency crews arrived from shore, as well as from our ship. Looking at Leo laid out on the dock; it was hard to believe we were talking to him just minutes earlier.

It felt like it took an hour before the fire department's rescue squad and ambulance arrived from town. I'm sure it was only minutes. At the same time, a squad car from the Two Harbors police pulled in to help direct traffic.

They worked on Leo for a few minutes, before loading him into the ambulance. Leo really didn't look good.

All of us stood around in shock. It is amazing how fast accidents happen.

As Leo was being transported to the local hospital's emergency room, the investigation of the accident started.

The Two Harbors police were joined by a squad from the county Sheriff's department, and between them and the foreman for the loading dock, questions were soon being asked. From what we could tell, it appeared to have been a freak dock accident.

The loading of ore into the ship had been delayed for over a half an hour. That meant that the departure time for the ship had been delayed as well. For the shipping company, that meant big money.

As they were interviewing Blackie and myself, asking questions about the accident, a call came in. Leo had died.

The officers were attempting to determine if it had been an accident or a homicide. A gloomy feeling fell over the dock. Everyone was in shock.

Because of Leo's death, the investigation took much longer than expected. The crew was tied up in the investigation most of the day. It was well after dark before we were loaded and allowed to leave.

The Two Harbor's police and Sheriff's Deputy Alex North wanted to talk to everyone in the area – both on-shore as well as those on the deck of the ship who might have witnessed the accident. While this was going on, the massive ore conveyor had been shut down.

Within the hour, a member of the Coast Guard arrived to review the situation as well, and make sure there wasn't any ship related conditions that had caused the accident.

So far, everything was still pointing to the fact that it was a terrible accident.

When Blackie and I went aboard ship, Captain Taccetta had a short meeting to make sure the entire crew knew the situation. He expressed his sorrow, and made sure we were all in the right frame of mind before resuming loading of ore. The last thing he wanted was another accident.

Meanwhile, the shipping company had sent word that they would have a temporary replacement for Leo by the time we reached our next port.

They would also send with him a Chaplin, so that we could have a service onboard for our departed member.

For now, it was the captain's duty to personally notify Leo's family.

He assumed the police had already notified the family. However, he wanted to explain how the crew was concerned about the family and how tragically his life ended. That was the least he could do.

Chapter 8

ID's

Agent Mark Lawson

It took a series of calls, but by the end of the next day, I had some answers. It was like pulling teeth to get the response that I had already suspected in the back of my mind. Dead man - with no relatives? That usually meant someone working undercover.

My call to the FBI Agent In-Charge in New Jersey, led to a series of phone calls made to the local police, DEA, and Immigration people. The agent had a hit with his call to ICE – Immigration and Customs Enforcement, and by afternoon, I was right in the middle of a long conversation with them.

"Why didn't you let us know about your man, when he went missing, and when the Sheriff pulled a search for him?" I asked the regional ICE agent. "And, if nothing else, couldn't you let our regional Special Agent for ICE know what you were doing?"

"We felt we had a leak. That's how they knew about our man. If we acknowledged him, they would have known for sure that they were being watched, and that they got our plant.

"Until we solve that problem, I can't let out additional information without compromising the operation. Let's just say, we have been working this case for over a year."

"Well, between you and me, that sounds like you had more than one person working the case."

"I cannot confirm what you said or deny it. However, you can't either. You need to hold any information to yourself unless we talk first."

After hanging up, I called the regional agent of the FBI in New Jersey and told him about the call I received.

"Sorry Mark, I knew about the operation, but I had agreed with them as well, that we would keep it under wraps. That's why I asked the ICE agent to call you directly."

I was not pleased with the results of my phone call. Unfortunately, there was little I could do.

New Jersey

The Special Agent In-Charge of the New Jersey FBI, Roy Hacket, had no sooner talked to Agent Mark Lawson when he received a call. It was from his counterpart Kyle Easton in the New Jersey ICE.

"I just got word that another one of our team on the Lake Superior Operation had an incident. We are checking into it, but we don't know if it was an act of assassination or an accident, Agent Easton told Agent Hacket.

"I just wanted you to know. We really do need to keep this operation under wraps. It's getting out of control. I'll call you in the morning with more details as we sort them out."

Roy Hacket, the New Jersey FBI agent was perplexed. Should he get Agent Lawson involved, or was the ICE agent right in keeping the wraps on the operation? So far, it looked as though someone else had more knowledge of the operation than ICE or the FBI had hoped they knew.

Minneapolis

In Minneapolis, FBI Agent Mark Lawson wondered what he should do next. He had promised the Sheriff that he would let him know if he found any information on the case.

Now, he knew the man had been working for ICE on a case. The exact facts about the case had not been disclosed, and he had been instructed by his fellow agent not to let others know.

This was not the normal method of investigation, and definitely not what had been preached at their regional meeting up in Duluth.

Mark decided it was time to run the communications problem up the ladder of responsibility. He made a call to his contact at Homeland Security, Agent Farley.

It was their task to make sure information was communicated between the agencies.

To Mark's surprise, the agent at Homeland Security told him he had just received a call from the New Jersey FBI Special Agent, and was reviewing the case. Even though he agreed that they needed to keep things under wraps, he wanted to set up an on-line video conference first thing tomorrow morning to discuss the case with FBI, ICE and Homeland Security offices in New Jersey and Minneapolis.

The management teams needed to know the facts to be able to react properly if and when anything surfaced.

Mark hung up the phone and simply shook his head. Wasn't that what all the communications meetings were all about? So much for paying attention.

The next morning, the Special Agents of the law enforcement agencies in the two territories were required to attend the video conference.

The agents from New Jersey were less than pleased how things were expanding. However, they were pleased that it was restrained to a few agents, and had not spread throughout the nation's law enforcement agencies.

Case discussion:

The following morning, Agent Farley of Homeland Security led the discussion for the video conference.

"I suppose most of you have heard about the smuggling case we solved in New York last year. It was part of Operation Lost Idol. It made most of the papers, and because of it, we sent a small splash out by means of our communications update email last year.

"According to the press, we raided several auction houses over the course of a week netting eight antiquities that were stolen overseas and were coming up for auction during Asia Week – New York. They called the raids a complete success.

"What you are going to hear today, I don't want repeated.

"It's the fact that the raids were not our intention. We have been investigating the smuggling of antiquities from Asia for over five years. ICE – Immigration and Customs Enforcement, has taken the lead in the U.S. What we found in New York was just a drop in the bucket from what we were trying to track. The goods we recovered from the auction houses were valued at almost a million dollars.

"The group we are attempting to track moves five times that amount every month. Every time we start to get close to the group, somehow they catch wind of our operation and change locations.

"The raid in New York last year was the result of a trucking company accidentally breaking open a shipping crate while it was in transit. When the crew spotted a bronze Buddha figurine that was obviously extremely old and valuable, they contacted a local beat patrol officer.

"Once it was reported, it forced our hand and we had to make it look as though we had cracked the case, and confiscated the stolen goods.

"It cost us six months of surveillance.

"This is an operation that is being tracked by England, France, China, India, Thailand, and the U.S.

"Thefts in China, India, and Pakistan are routed through Thailand and Hong Kong to the American, English, and French auction houses. About 2,500 items were confiscated in the past eight years before we realized how big the operation was.

"When one jewel showed up that was worth around $1.3 million, agents from China started working with us to track down the smugglers.

"Typically, most of the goods show up in private placement auctions, which are difficult to spot.

"Every once in a while, the goods show up in a public auction. Usually these goods have already been smuggled in, and had been sold to private collections. The new owner usually picks them up for a good price, and attempt to resell the goods as family treasures.

"The million-dollars worth of goods we confiscated, was only a small fraction of the almost 400-million dollars they auctioned off that week. It's hard to track the legitimacy of all those sales. Most of them were legit.

"We have been cooperating with other governments attempting to stop this major ring of smugglers. Take my word for it; it is hard to determine where the goods are going once they enter the US.

"Our agent, who was attempting to work undercover in the Duluth harbor for the past year, was discovered shot in his vehicle in northern Wisconsin last week. Agent Mark Lawson, I believe you and a couple other law enforcement agents discovered his body in his car.

"He had worked on the case for three years along the wharfs of New York and New Jersey.

"What he was tracking, was the delivery of small antiquities by international shipping. More specifically, lately he was tracking several shipments from Canadian ports to U.S. ports in Chicago, Milwaukee, and Duluth. As soon as we spotted a pattern, the smugglers would change their locations.

"The other trick the smugglers used was smuggling a fake item. A small dark-green glass item looks very similar to a jade item. If our agents got too close, they would openly ship the fake item with just enough covering to see if we would take the bait, letting them know we were on to their methods.

"We have teams in L.A., San Francisco, Seattle, Duluth, New York, and Miami working on the case.

"So, don't feel left out. This is a case many people have worked on for a long time, and we are close.

"Unfortunately, losing Bo Callahan has set us back. It looked as though someone lured him out there for a meeting, and shot him as he drove by.

"There was another "accident" this week in Two Harbors. We are not sure if it was intentional or an accident, but a heavy maintenance bucket swung off the loading dock, striking a crewmember, knocking him into the water. He died an hour later.

"We figured that his ship was one of the ships carrying the stolen goods that week.

"That's it in a nutshell. We have put a lot of work into this one, and just as we were about to ring it in, it appears that they are getting inside information about our operation. I need your support as well as silence as we attempt to put the final cap on this case.

"We want to catch the whole operation, not just one of the smugglers. We think we are close.

"There has been a great deal of cooperation from our counterparts in Asia as well as Europe. We are tired of the courts giving someone a six-month sentence for smuggling when the whole group needs to be sent away for a long time.

"Mark, since you sniffed our case out, we have a request for you. One of your fellow bird hunters investigated the death of a seaman earlier this week in Two Harbors. Since the FBI had not been involved in the death, I think it would be a good excuse for you, and, let's see, Deputy North, to interview the crewmembers of the ship, when it gets back into port.

"I'm not sure if this is its last trip for the Calvin Wroth, or if it has one more trip back to Two Harbors. However, the Calvin Wroth's next set of cargo trips are going to be from Duluth.

"I'd like to have you determine whether it was murder, or a bad accident.

"You might have to let Deputy North know why you are butting into her inquiry, but I think you can figure out a way to handle it quietly.

"Any questions?"

Agent Mark Lawson

After our discussion, I had a chance to review my thoughts.

There were a few specific questions that were asked. However, it was obvious; we were touching but a small spoke of their operation. That was why the agents in the other regions were not involved in the conference call. Without knowing where the leak was, he was keeping everything to a "need to know" basis, including who was working on the case.

He never did let me know if they had contacted the Sheriff and informed him of the fact that it was their agent. My guess was they had not.

I felt like I was starting to get better at reading between the lines on this case.

I put a call into Deputy Alex North. I needed to review her notes from the Two Harbors accident, and quickly set up a meeting with her when the Calvin Wroth returned to port in Two Harbors.

Chapter 9

Coincidence?

Alex North returned my call a little later that day.

"Mark, this is Deputy Alex North, you left me a message to call you as quickly as possible. What's up? Did you get a lead on the shooter in Wisconsin?"

"Well, we're still working on that one. I had another question for you. I understand you investigated the death of a seaman from the Calvin Wroth this week. Since the boat transports its crew from state to state, I've been asked to review the case.

"Can you tell me about it? Also, do you know when the boat is due back in port?"

Alex told me about the accident; and how a bucket filled with bolts swung from high above the loading dock, hitting the seaman in the head – knocking him into the water.

"Do you think it was an accident?" I asked her.

"It would have taken a great shot to do it on purpose," she told me. "You ever try swinging a fifty-foot rope, and hit someone with it?"

"When are they due back in port?" I inquired.

"Tomorrow, sometime. Let's see, the Shipping News says 2 pm. I think the captain told me they have one more run to Sault Ste. Marie. Why?"

"I'll explain later. For now, I need to have the two of us interview several crewmembers as well as a few dockworkers. I'll be up there in the morning.

"Can you clear your schedule?"

"I was hoping you wanted to go deer hunting." She said in jest. "Sure, I'll call the Sheriff and let him know I'm meeting you."

"Can you leave my name out, and tell him you missed a couple crew members that might have observed the accident? I'll explain when I get there."

We arranged a meeting at the parking lot by the lighthouse. I told her I would pick up donuts on the way up if she picked up the coffee.

Calvin Wroth – Lake Superior

Captain Taccetta was informed by the home office of his shipping company that the FBI wanted to interview his crew, when they made port in Two Harbors, prior to unloading.

They asked him to adjust his schedule and to set up a place for FBI Agent Lawson to meet and talk to the crew.

The captain was not pleased to hear that once again he would be delaying the shipping operations. It was almost impossible for him to make the time back up in transit.

"What are they looking for?" he asked. "I thought that they concluded it was an accident?"

"We agree. However, since the FBI was not there, they want a chance to say they were part of the inquiry.

"Just make them happy."

As a result of the request, Captain Taccetta adjusted his port schedule, adding an extra two hours to the ships planned stay in Two Harbors.

Two Harbors, Minnesota

When I arrived in Two Harbors, Alex was sitting in her cruiser watching the seagulls in the parking lot as well as out in the harbor. For once, I was glad I was right on time – she had the hot coffee.

I motioned to her to join me in my car.

When she did, she asked, "Okay, what's so important that you didn't want anyone in my department to know I was meeting with you, and we had to meet out here in the harbor?"

"What do you mean? It's a sunny day and the scenery is great. Don't you have meetings out here all the time? If this was my territory, I sure would. It definitely beats a dark dreary conference room."

After telling her that everything I was about to tell her could not show up in her daily notes, I told Alex the information about the dead man from our hunting trip.

"I still have no idea who killed him or why. But, ICE thinks he was getting too close on an investigation, and they wanted him out of the way.

"Apparently, they also have a lead on the Calvin Wroth, and they want us to go through the motions of concluding an investigation.

"We contacted the shipping company and they are expecting me when they bring the boat in."

"Well, if you are planning on talking to them, you better clean up a few items," she told me. "Unless you are planning on taking it out to go fishing, you might want to call it a ship, not a boat. They get their spines up when someone doesn't know the difference. In addition, who are you planning to talk to? I talked to everyone last time."

"I know. We needed to make up an excuse that I am re-confirming their stories, so we can both be there. We'll need to talk to three or four from the dock as well in order to make the story hold true."

"I suppose you can't tell me the rest of the story," she told me.

"You'd have to shoot me first. However, after watching how you missed the only pheasant dumb enough to fly in front of us, I guess I'm not too worried. You think you can make up a story for the Sheriff why you were busy today?"

"Already got it covered."

After finishing our donuts and coffee, we drove back to the loading dock to talk to the foreman and two maintenance people.

Between the three dockworkers, their story was just like Alex had told me. Alex didn't notice any wavering of the story between the first time and today.

Both the maintenance workers that were up high on the ore terminal, fixing a pulley on the ore belt, and the assistant that was on the ground, swore that it was the first time the bucket had fallen, and that there had been no chance for a practice swing. It was simply an accident. It had been tied to a beam that extended out from the ore dock, and the worker had moved down the conveyor about thirty feet from where he started working.

I hadn't realized how brutally the bucket had struck the crewman. Alex had the photos of the dead man. She was right; trying to hit one person at that range would have taken a lot of practice and timing. According to the crew, this was the first time the bucket had slipped off the work ledge.

Trying to hit someone on the first try sounded next to impossible.

To make it look like a good investigation, I asked the maintenance worker to fill a bucket with bolts and attach a rope, just as he had done the day of the accident.

Then, he and I went up on the dock, leaving Alex below, near the spot of the accident.

The rope was fifty feet long, and the ledge was about fifty-three feet high. There was a beam that protruded out about two feet that had an eyebolt on it. That was where the rope had been attached. When the bucket was lowered, it would be about three feet from the ground, so his assistant could detach it, and send it up with the required materials.

Finally, the final spot he was working on looked like it was fifty feet from the ramp.

"Just walk slowly along on the ramp towards the dock, I told Alex. Make sure you are watching the bucket. We don't want it to hit you."

Alex slowly walked up the ramp to the dock.

As she was almost at the spot the accident happened, I let the bucket swing.

"Look out," I shouted.

To her surprise, it was close enough that Alex had to duck to make sure the bucket would not crack her skull open like the poor victim.

"Hey, that was close. You sure you weren't trying to hit me?" she asked. "Just remember, I'd have to tell my Sheriff who hit me."

It was a good test. I really didn't think I could get that close on the first attempt. I decided to play it safe and not make any more attempts. I didn't want to accidentally hit Alex. Besides, the dockworkers had guaranteed us there had not been any practice swings. Someone would have noticed it.

I realized that with a little physics, it would have told me the time it would take the bucket to drop fifty-feet. It was simply a calculation of gravity. One could easily look it up online.

In the old days, when I was in college, I had to calculate similar problems by hand.

Just under two-seconds was my quick calculation. So, how far would a person walk in one and one-half seconds? At the slow pace of walking on the ramp, not very far.

It was possible…

I treated Alex to lunch while we waited for the ship to come in.

We found a quiet booth and discussed the possibility that the seaman might have been hit intentionally by the heavy bucket.

Alex had dismissed it originally. However, after cruising the bucket over her head earlier on my first try, she was starting to wonder if her first impression of the possibility of it being an accident was correct.

"You know, I heard you shout, "look out" real clear. I wonder how they heard it with the big conveyor running?" Alex commented.

The discussion led to a couple good questions:
Who were they trying to hit?
Were they trying to kill him or injure him?
What if they missed?

Finally, how did the dockworkers know which of the seamen would be leaving the ship on their supply run to Shopko and Super One Foods that day?

Chapter 10

Interviews

The Calvin Wroth was pulling into port right on schedule. We stood there with the terminal foreman waiting for the ship to tie up so Alex and I could go onboard.

When the ship was securely tied up, Captain Taccetta met us at the gangway and escorted us up to one of the meeting rooms.

He told us, "You can use this room if you would like to talk to my crew. It is secluded so you will not be disturbed. I'll have my 2nd Mate, Joe Labonta, outside the door to bring whomever you would like.

"Deputy North, I believe you have the list of those you talked to earlier that might have observed anything. If you have any questions or problems, please let me know.

"I'm sure my crew will cooperate with whatever you need. They are still in shock from the sudden death of 3rd Mate Leo Brasso last trip. He was well liked by everyone."

I gave the list to the 2nd Mate. There were eight people on the list who had been in a position that could have observed anything on shore. I requested that he call the men in order, with Blackie and Stubby bringing up the end of the list.

Since we had already talked to the two dockworkers earlier, I was looking for any minor variances in the story.

The first person we interviewed was a deck hand that was supervising the loading of supplies. From his location on the top deck, everything was visible. The only problem, he was paying attention to his job and not the crew coming back from town.

He told us that his first indication that something was wrong was when, out of the side of his eyes, he spotted 3rd Mate Brasso hit the water with a big splash. With that, he radioed the alarm to the bridge.

At that time, he did not realize why Brasso had fallen into the water. When he saw that he was not moving, he stopped the loading of a pallet of supplies, and ran down to see if there was anything he could do.

Up until that point, the deck hand had not spotted anything out of the ordinary on the dock.

As we went down the list of people to interview, everyone had a version close to the same story. They had noticed nothing unusual on the ore terminal until they heard a shout and saw Brasso in the water.

One of the men saw the group from the Calvin Wroth arrive. He stated that he glanced away just before the accident.

It wasn't until they interviewed Blackie that they heard a different and more detailed description of what happened.

Blackie gave them the whole story.

"We got our lists from each of our departments, toothpaste, deodorant and a few other minor things. Brasso, Stubby and I took the normal run to the Shopko and Super One Foods to pick up the supplies the crew requested. It didn't take us long; the lists were short on this trip.

"The car and driver took us directly to the store, and about forty-five minutes later we came back out with the four bags of items we had purchased.

"Like I said, it didn't take us very long.

"On the way back, we paused for a couple minutes at the old locomotives, so that Stubby could see how big the old steam engines were that used to haul the ore to the docks. Then, we came directly back to the ore dock."

"Nothing out of the ordinary up to that point?" I asked Blackie. "How many times have you done that run?"

"Well, as low man on the engineering totem pole, probably ten times. Occasionally, one of the other engineers wants to get off the ship to stretch their legs. But otherwise, I'm running the errands. It felt like another run to the store."

"OK, take us through the point where all of you were on the ramp to the dock. Don't leave anything out, even if it was a seagull flying low to check out your bags," I told Blackie.

"Well, when we got out of the car, I grabbed one bag, Stubby grabbed two and 3rd Mate Brasso grabbed the other one. I think the deck hand's list was the longest and that's why Stubby had the two bags.

"We walked down to the ramp and then walked single file to the dock as there were a few boxes on the ramp.

"I remembered telling the others not to trip on the boxes. I'm not sure what was in them, but my guess was parts for the ore terminal repair.

"I gave a wave to our deck hand up on the ship that was loading supplies. Then, I glanced back at the boxes on the ramp.

Brasso was in the lead, like normal. The officers always were in the lead coming back to the ship.

"Then, there was Stubby and myself.

"As we were close to the end of the ramp, I heard a faint "look out" that was muffled by all the noise of the terminal's conveyor. That's when I spotted it out of the corner of my eye.

"A rusty old supply bucket, on a rope, was swinging right towards us on the end of the ramp. It must have been bumped from the top of the terminal where they were working.

"I think I shouted, "duck," and grabbed Stubby by the arm or shoulder. I can't remember for sure. He lost his balance and fell backward. I remember my bag and the bags that Stubby was carrying dumping all over the ramp.

"I don't think Brasso heard me, or he was slow to react. When the bucket hit him in the head, his bag dropped right there and he hit the water as if he was doing a belly flop.

"It happened so fast, I didn't have a chance to push him out of the way.

"I thought he would climb back up and give someone hell for knocking him off the dock. Then I realized, he wasn't moving.

"We got him up on the dock, but there was nothing we could do for him. His head was in bad shape.

"That's all I remember," Blackie told Deputy North and me.

"Had your group slowed down or stopped at the end of the ramp?" I asked.

"Perhaps. There was a small step. I suppose with our bags we might have slowed down a fraction to make sure we didn't trip as we stepped on the dock."

Blackie's story followed the original story extremely close. If he knew the bucket was coming, he hadn't let it slip. You could tell by the sound of his voice, that the incident was still affecting him.

We thanked him for taking the time to re-tell the story. The last one on the list was Stubby O'Shea.

As Blackie left the conference room, Stubby O'Shea entered the room and closed the door behind him.

"Well, Stubby, I'm FBI Special Agent Mark Lawson, and you met Deputy Alex North a few days ago.

"I'm glad to meet you. Sounds to me like you're the luckiest man on this ship, or someone was sending you one hell of a strong warning."

Chapter 11

"One" Second

Stubby had a surprised look in his eyes as I told him he was either the luckiest man on this ship, or someone was sending him one hell of a strong warning. It caught Deputy North by surprise as well.

"So, what's your thought? Were you the target, or were they sending a message and wanted to see how everyone would react?"

It took Stubby a second, but looking at us, he started to realize I was not here to interrogate him.

"How did you know?" Stubby asked.

"Deputy North and I were attending a conference in Duluth a short while ago. After the conference, four of us went pheasant hunting.

"As it turned out, we were first at the scene of a shooting just south of Superior. Man shot execution style with a handgun as he drove down a gravel road. I guess I've seen too many cases of unidentifiable people that appeared to have been ambushed. In addition, I suppose I asked too many questions about who the man was. Reluctantly, they told me the whole story.

"Trust me, it took some teeth pulling. Since Deputy North was incidentally here on this call as well, I figured she could be a help in the investigation. Her Sheriff doesn't even know, yet. She is simply assisting me today on my "official" investigation.

"Everyone on the dock and ship thinks this is simply an FBI follow-up investigation of the accident.

"So, Stubby, what's your take on this: Accident? Attempted murder? Or, someone was testing to see if there was an agent on board?"

"You talked to everyone, what's your guess?" he asked.

"From what I've heard, and the results of a simple test we ran this morning with swinging a bucket from the loading dock, I'd say you were one second from being dead. If Blackie hadn't grabbed you and shouted, "Look out," Brasso wouldn't have paused for a second on the ramp before reacting, and the bucket would have swung right behind him. My guess is - right about where you should have been.

"I think they would have been fishing you out of the cold water instead of him," I suggested.

Stubby gave a squint and a slight shake of his head. "That was my guess as well. The bucket was full. Nothing could have been taken out of it prior to it falling. It was as heavy as it could have been. I'm not betting on it being an accident, I've seen too many of those accidents on the docks in Jersey.

"So, what brings you onboard, and what's your place at the table?" Stubby asked. "Does anyone else know?"

"So far, no one knows. We have about the fifteen minutes we gave to Blackie to talk to you before anyone becomes suspicious. As of now, we are staying out of your investigation and looking into the shore activities of the group to see if we can find the links.

"Someone told the dock workers you were heading off the ship. Same with your man in Superior. We want to find the communications and try to get a leg up on them. Meanwhile, I'll keep track of your ship's movements. If you need support, Deputy North or I will only be a call away. We just wanted to let you know we were working behind the scenes on this case."

"I appreciate the help. Just make sure no one knows or you'll find me floating somewhere in Lake Superior."

"That's our job. You stay safe. I'll be talking with your boss, in ICE, as well. Unfortunately, I think our time's about up.

"We will conclude that it was a terrible accident. Your captain will have our complete report."

With that, we shook Stubby's hand and sent him on his way back to his post.

I asked the 2nd Mate, Joe Labonta, to show us to the captain.

When we were escorted to the bridge, we explained that the accident appeared to be a "one of a kind" happening, and unfortunately, three people were in the way of a falling bucket. There was no evidence to the contrary.

I thanked him for the delay, and told him that it appeared to me that everyone on the ship as well as the crew on shore was in the clear.

Deputy North and I headed back down the gangplank to the dock, and then back to our car.

As we did, we kept an eye open for anyone that might have been paying a little more than normal attention to us. I was sure someone was monitoring every move we made. Actually, I was hoping it was the case. We needed someone to make a mistake. This was going be a tough case to crack.

Alex asked, "You knew Stubby was an agent?"

"Actually, no! I figured it out today. Let's go find a quiet place we can talk."

Alex and I drove to a restaurant a few miles north of town to sit and discuss the day. It would be quiet there this time of day, and we could make sure no one else was there that might be keeping an eye on us. Besides, their dining room had a great view of the lake.

As we drove, I told her how I figured out Stubby was an agent.

"I was told that we had an agent on the Calvin Wroth and that there had been an accident. They didn't say that our agent had been killed. Since Brasso and Blackie had been on the boat for several years, that left Stubby.

"New guy from Jersey, just like our man in Wisconsin. It had to be him. It was an educated guess."

"And you didn't tell me?"

"I needed the element of surprise. Did you notice Stubby checking out our expressions?"

As we arrived at the restaurant, I tried to fill her in on what I learned about the man shot in his car in Wisconsin. I had to be careful not to say more than I felt I was allowed to by the agents in New Jersey.

I knew Alex must have had a list of questions going through her mind as to what was going on.

"Can you give me a little hint as to what our role is going to be in this case?" Alex asked.

"Good question. Since I've been told under no uncertain terms this is an ICE case, as I told Stubby, I think we need to stick to on-shore intelligence.

"If we can find a link from someone on the docks to the ship or another dock location, we might be able to assist them. I'm guessing that will be part of my job for now.

"I think you need to tell your boss that you assisted me in my investigation, and we also discussed the shooting we uncovered in Wisconsin. He should understand that it took most of the day.

"I still don't know what it is that they are smuggling into the country. I'm sure we will know when it is time to round them up.

"For now, this is a wait and see game. Until then, keep your ears open to any friends that might have heard anything more than what we have officially released about the dock accident. A slight slip of the tongue might be the lead we need. Someone knew who was leaving the ship and was all set for them."

I was hoping that Alex could handle the limited info role that I had just led her into.

I wouldn't want to be the deer that crossed her path in the next day. She would have probably used a cannon on it to release the stress she was building up over this case.

As we were about to leave the restaurant, we spotted the Calvin Wroth heading out on the lake. It had finished loading and was heading east to deliver its load of iron ore. Hopefully, Stubby would be safe and our interrogation would make it look as though he was just another seaman.

On the way back to my office in Minneapolis, I put a call in to the Sheriff's Department in Douglas County, Wisconsin. I was lucky, Rick Bernaski the Douglas County Sheriff was in his office.

"Rick, this is FBI Special Agent Mark Lawson. I was thinking about our individual that was shot on that gravel road. When you brought in his car to check for fingerprints, did you happen to find a cell phone anywhere in his car?"

"Yes, we did. The only problem is that one of the agents in Customs Enforcement showed up and took control of all our evidence. He had a paper saying it was a Federal Case and they would pick up the investigation."

I laughed. For an organization that did not want to let anyone know about their presence in the case, they were leaving clues all over the place.

"Thanks Rick. I'll handle it through Minneapolis. I was hoping we might get some clues from the phone, as to who was in contact with the deceased. Your people didn't accidentally get a chance to look it over before they took it, did you?"

"Barely. We didn't even get a chance to write the numbers down before they swooped in on my office. We did get the phone number and had it checked for prints. Hope you have better luck."

"Thanks, I'll let you know if I find anything. Can you text me the phone number. Hopefully, it will give me a start."

With that, I hung up and called the Agent In Charge of the regional Customs Offices in Minneapolis. I told him that I needed to meet with him, and we set up a meeting for the next morning.

Meanwhile, I put a call in to my office. I asked my assistant to pull the cell phone records from the local towers for the dockworkers, which I had on my interview list, for the week prior to the accident, as well as those from the group I interviewed on the ship.

I was hoping to find a common phone number between them. I figured the request would take a day or two. Looking for that needle in a haystack usually takes time. There was no guarantee that they used a registered phone either.

The rest of the way to Minneapolis, I tried to figure out what to say to the agent over at Customs, in order to convince him to let me examine the deceased man's phone.

The next morning, first thing, I had my meeting with Agent Olson from Customs. I explained that death investigations of my two victims fell under FBI jurisdiction. I was planning to stay out of their larger investigation, but at the same time, I was planning on working behind the scenes to see if we could find any links to implicate the shooter.

After a convincing argument on my part, and not allowing him the time to talk to New Jersey to get their opinion first, he agreed to send me a copy of the phone and text records from the deceased.

However, he did leave one contingency. I had to agree to discuss any actions we took, with him, before we moved on the case.

I knew I was playing a long shot at best anyway, so I agreed to work with him. For now, the phone records could be traced, and crosschecked, against the phone records from Two Harbors. It would be easier for our department to accomplish this task than the Custom's group. If we did find any connections, I knew I would be talking with the agents in New Jersey anyway. Either way, it was a productive meeting.

Heading back to my office, I checked to see if I had any urgent requests on any of the other cases we were handling.

Chapter 12

Shipments

<u>Hong Kong</u>

A package arrived by courier at the twelfth floor offices of the Chen-Lee Tea Company. It was a small office in the seventeen-story tower and was used by the company to receive and ship orders from their many warehouses to customers. Unlike other package deliveries, the courier did not leave it with the secretary or ask for a signature.

The secretary pushed a button located on the bottom of her desk letting her boss know someone was coming. The security camera located in the lobby showed him who it was. After getting the nod from the secretary, the courier carried the package directly to the office of the manager.

As the manager opened the door, he greeted the courier with a broad smile. "You have my request?" he asked.

The courier smiled back. "Yes, your order is safe and secure," he stated, as he gently set the package on his desk. "And, you have something for me as well?"

The manager reached in to his desk drawer and withdrew a large envelope. "As we agreed," he told him. "Please tell your people that I may have a few more requests later this month. I will send them the list. Hopefully, they will be just as successful locating the items we are looking for."

"We will be awaiting your list. Have a good day."

With that, the courier put the envelope in the inside pocket of his jacket and left the office. His job was completed. The discussion had been kept to a formal minimal amount and the transaction completed without prying eyes.

As the manager watched the security camera, waiting for evidence that the courier had left the offices, he got up and locked his door. In front of him was the prize delivery he had been waiting for. It had been two months in the planning. Gently, he opened the package to check out the merchandise.

The package was heavy and he did not want to take any chances of dropping it. As he slowly opened the box and unwrapped its contents, which were well wrapped in bubble wrap, he stood there in amazement. There it was; a jade Buddha from a temple in Bhutan, just over the Himalayan Mountains from China. It was only six inches high, but values rarely are proportional to size. In this case, the nearly 2000-year-old statue would be worth well over $400,000 to the right buyer.

To the uneducated eye, it probably looked like just another Buddha statue as you might find in any of the bazaars. However, this one could be traced back to the year 47 BC. Made from Imperial jade, it was one of the most sought-after forms of antique carvings. The surface of the white nephrite carving was almost translucent. The inclusions of a dark russet color in the jade was so well planned into the final product that they appeared to have been painted onto the surface. Only a true master cutter could have crafted such a fine statue, and that was why it had been in a temple for all these years.

Actually, it was one of several statues that were created in India in 43 BC in the city of Pataliputra. In the 4th century AD, they were to be moved by Buddhist monks, to save them from a war. They were to be transported to Sri Lanka and eventually to Thailand. The largest of the statues was moved to Bangkok's Wat Phra Kaew in 1779, to the Temple of the Emerald Buddha, located within the grounds of the Grand Palace. There the large Buddha statue is ceremoniously clothed by the King of Thailand at the changing of each season with gold plated robes.

Records showed that there were two smaller statues. Some theorize that they were models for the larger and more intricate statue. Apparently, they were lost in the move. Rumors of their locations have been floating around for almost a hundred years. Some say they were sent to Temples along the way as payment for safe passage of the larger Buddha to Bangkok.

Earlier this year, when one of the jade statues floated onto the black market, there was a bidding war that was never seen on anyone's books.   It was so valuable that two of the bidders disappeared just before the final offer was negotiated, never to be seen again.

This jade Buddha's stop in Hong Kong was just a temporary stop on the way to a wealthy buyer in Vancouver, Canada. It was to be packaged as a cheap piece of common jade and listed with a retail price of only six dollars. Passage through customs would be easy, since the real identification of the object would not be shown on the invoice. Only a true expert would be able to spot that it was not a cheap statue produced in the many jade factories in Thailand. Even the seal on the bottom of the statue indicated a company in Thailand had manufactured the statue.

Once the manager was convinced it was the authentic statue and not a replica, he repackaged it and shipped it to his contact in Vancouver. Then, in a private transaction, the statue would be sold to an antiquities expert who was aware of the real significance of the object.

All along, import taxes and antiquities laws would be ignored. If someone in Customs were made aware of the shipment, huge fines and imprisonment would follow the rightful return of the Buddha to the Temple of the Emerald Buddha. It was a risky operation; however, it was with great rewards. If anything happened to the Buddha, the company would be out a sizeable amount of money. However, by sending it by standard shipping, if the customs authorities discovered it, it would be hard to prove that anyone at the Chen-Lee Tea Company knew it was a treasure and that they should be prosecuted. They were simply shipping a trinket to a customer. The calculated risks to the company were always on the top of the list when a contract was initiated with the "organization."

By the end of the week, the shipment and transactions were complete with the delivery to its final destination. Housed in a freshly built bulletproof glass display in a private room, the new owner admired his new acquisition. The quality of the carving by the stone artists used in creating the statue was amazing.

Unfortunately, this statue would rarely be seen again.

This had been one of many unique items sold in the past few years by the "organization." In some cases, they had discovered rare items that were up for sale in Asia. In others, wealthy collectors had given them a list of items they would like to procure. Exactly how the "organization" obtained the merchandise was not discussed. Only the quality and final price were the determining factors.

The "organization" had developed many contacts throughout Asia, including developing a network to ship items to distributors located in North America and Europe. However, it had been the U.S. market that created the largest demand for their items.

To avoid detection, the "organization" had developed shipping routes through several cities including Vancouver, San Diego, Toronto, Miami and New York. It made the magnitude of the shipments harder to spot or track. Even when one of their shipments was accidentally discovered in New York last year, it appeared that Customs had decided it was a single shipment, and they had failed to discover the size of their "organization."

Just a few weeks earlier this month, they had shipped a rare manuscript from China through Toronto, on its way to the U.S. It was as though they could ship anything they wanted as long as they kept the quantity down and locations separate.

With this shipment completed, it was time to concentrate on the next item, which was expected to be routed through their Hong Kong offices of the Chen-Lee Tea Company. This time, they were expecting to receive a package that originated from North Korea.

Even though North Korea had some of the tightest restriction on goods shipped from the country, their contacts assured the "organization" that they could supply the requested items.

It was indeed a risky business. In North Korea, if they were caught, they would spend life in prison, provided they were not hung by a rope or shot by a firing squad as an example to other smugglers. Their trial would be short, with a verdict that was determined long before any formal trial.

Chapter 13

Monitoring

New Jersey

The office of Customs and Homeland Security's switchboard was ablaze with phone calls. When the news reached them that FBI Special Agent Mark Lawson and Deputy North had made contact with Stubby O'Shea, hairs on the back of their necks were already standing on end.

"What didn't he understand from our conversation last week," the Customs Agent Easton told Agent Farley of Homeland Security.

Agent Farley tried to calm him down. "Relax, so far he is doing exactly what we told him to do. We have two dead people. We need to find their killers. As long as he makes it look as though he is investigating the murders, and not the smuggling, we're clear – understand?"

"You think he can be trusted?"

"Yes, I have had conversations with his boss. He told me that Agent Lawson was as good as he had in the field. If it will make you feel more comfortable, I'll contact him and drop another reminder on him, to give the case a wide berth. He'll understand."

The Customs Agent was not totally convinced. However, there was very little he could do at this point to keep FBI Agent Mark Lawson out of the case.

When Agent Easton got off the phone, he called FBI Special Agent Lawson, hoping to confer and make sure there weren't any conflicts that would jeopardize their case.

"Agent Lawson, Agent Farley from Homeland here. I hear you have been busy. Thought we should touch base."

"Agent Farley, I was wondering how long it would take before I got a call from someone on the east coast. What can I do for you?" he responded.

"Well Mark, not a lot. Just trying to keep everyone in their lanes and not worrying about the other person. I hear you touched base with Stubby O'Shea, and you are checking phone call links. Anything there?"

"I won't know for a few days. I just got the cell phone list from the killing in Wisconsin. It will take a little while to cross-link it with cell towers and the Two Harbors case.

"I figured, if we made it look like an official investigation into the accident in Two Harbors, it might take some observation off Stubby. Besides, this way we have more cell tower signals we can check after our presence up there. Maybe we can find a link. You don't suppose someone might call their people after the FBI visit?"

"Okay, Agent Lawson, I see your madness. Do me a favor; call me if you find anything. We may want to refigure how we want to bring down this organization."

"Sure. By the way, if you want everything secret, having Customs mysteriously claim all the evidence in Wisconsin probably was not the best of methods. You would have been better off letting me pull the case and leave it as a random shooting."

"Touché. I'll drop the hint to Customs here in New Jersey. Someday, we will get this machine all oiled up and running smoothly.

"Wish I could show you the whole picture. This one is very complicated. Meanwhile, keep in touch if you see anything related to the case you are working on or hear any rumors."

"I'll do that Agent Farley. Let Customs know they can share any info they find as well."

Agent Mark Lawson

I was wondering how long it would take before I got a phone call from the east coast. I was hoping that Agent Easton would drop a little more information on me as to what was going down. Whatever it was, trying to keep two deaths silent was not our normal style, at least within the agencies.

Alex North had sent me a text message from her personal phone. She said that her Sheriff had let our visit to Two Harbors go as just a follow-up investigation.

Since then, she had talked to the local police in Two Harbors and asked them to keep an ear open to anyone that seemed to know more than what was officially released.

Her hope was that someone would open their mouth at one of the bars and the story might spread until one of the deputies might pick up on the loose chatter from someone that had overheard the conversation.

So far, this case was starting to take a life of its own. I was concerned that we were giving it too much of our effort without knowing the real story. We had other cases to solve. The problem was; when someone feeds you one piece of candy, you want to see where they got it, and if they hid the rest.

As soon as I was done mulling over the situation, one of our agents called. He got a strong lead on the bank robbery we were pursuing. I was glad to hear it. Our agents had been pursuing that case for two weeks and we had been following up on a number of leads. This one looked as though it might lead us to the actual robber.

It kept my mind off the Custom's case the rest of the day and most of the next. With the aid of the local police, we picked up our suspect, got a search warrant, and recovered some of the stolen bank money from another location.

It took a while for us to complete and review the paperwork after our arrest. It felt good to be able to take one thing off the board.

The next day, I reviewed the analysis of the phone logs from Wisconsin and Two Harbors with one of my agents, who had been checking the lists as well as the cell tower's logs for phone number and text links.

The analysis took a lot of time. There were no links seen between the Wisconsin incident and the Two Harbors incident.

However, in each case there was a phone call made to Toronto. It was a different number in each case. Then again, it was a possible lead. Each time the phones were used, they were unregistered burner phones.

I thanked the agent for the effort, and we put an alert on the phone numbers used from Wisconsin as well as the one in Two Harbors.

Right now, it appeared that both of the phones GPS locators had been turned off. To do that, someone would have had to remove the batteries. If they put them to use again, hopefully, we could start tracking their locations.

Chapter 14

The China Caper

Background Information

During the period of years between 618 to 906 AD, China started to open up its influences throughout the region. It was a period that saw diplomacy, conquest, trade and pilgrimage. These years were marked in history under the Tang Dynasty. It was one of the greatest empires of the time.

For almost 300 years, China's power was centered around the ancient city of Chang'an, which is the present day Chinese city of Xi'an. Merchants and envoys from India, Korea, Japan, Persia, Mongolia, and Arabia could be seen in the streets. As a result, it was a period marked with cultural exchange with the outside world.

Towards the end of this period, China flourished in painting and classical writing. The values of Confucianism are found in the scrolls and paintings from the period.

Most of the advances found in the Tang Dynasty's culture slowed near the end of the ninth century, when China decided that most religions were to be banned. Many religions were present in China at the time (Christianity, Manichaeism, and Zoroastrianism). However, the strong Buddhist legacy, which had been carried from China to Korea and Japan, and brought pagodas and icons to those countries, now found itself included in the banned religions by China.

The result of all of the changes was a weakened Chinese government and turmoil within the country. Now, China was open to raids by border bandits. The Tang Dynasty was crumbling from within.

With the raids on rare treasures and with its religious groups attempting to move their treasured icons, literature and drawings to safer locations, many of the treasures ended up in the surrounding countries.

Almost a thousand years later, following the end of World War II, this cultural upheaval was further complicated with the creation of the communist nation of North Korea.

The division of the Koreas on approximately the 38th parallel was a division that was agreed on as an attempt to keep Russia from taking over the whole country. The country had been under Japanese control prior to the war.

The Korean War, which followed years later, was a further attempt by North Korea and Russia to push the U.S. out of South Korea. Russia supported North Korea financially and supplied the arms that kept North Korea fighting.

After several years of fighting, the old divisional line near the 38th parallel was once again firmly established as the dividing line between North and South Korea.

The north was under the control of a dictatorship that stayed in complete control for many years. Under this leadership, communist principles were in effect and the prosperity of the nation started to crumble by the 1990's due to huge loans from the USSR and a lack of infrastructure, including agriculture.

Religions, which flourished in South Korea, were officially discouraged in North Korea, and the writings of the leaders condemned the religions for their influences.

As a result, by 2010, most of the churches and temples remained only as architectural reminders of the past. Many of the artifacts were confiscated by the state or went underground; hoping for the day the nation would change its leadership.

The extreme isolationism of the country, which followed, prevented even the bringing of religious writings into the country. With the threats of starvation, the country turned its military into a world threat in order for the country to receive recognition and to bargain for food. Trade, as exhibited by other nations of the world, essentially stopped. The government was in control, and everything else was prohibited.

When a nation has strict controls and poverty, it usually brings on the black market. Individuals balance the risks of imprisonment or death against the chance for monetary rewards or freedom and security for their families.

Word slipped through the cracks of the regime, reaching the outside world, that there was a possibility of obtaining some of the treasures of the Tang Dynasty. They had been kept hidden from the world as part of the secret treasures of the North Korean government. Interest picked up quickly.

How someone would get it out of North Korea was not the concern. However, if someone did get some of the treasures out of the country, it definitely would create a bidding war for the articles.

For anyone brave enough to attempt to smuggle items out of North Korea, there was the additional risk to their families, including the risk of imprisonment or death. If caught, the person's family would probably find themselves in a work prison for the remainder of their lives. It was a threat to the North Korean population that had been carried out many times in the past.

The prison systems in North Korea are known for atrocious conduct. Once inside, all human rights are ignored. Torture, starvation, and other types of conduct are common in these institutions.

It was almost three months ago, that word was picked up by the "organization" that a rare Tang Dynasty drawing was available if the price was right. For a country where the population worked for a minimum wage of 65,000 North Korean Won – KPW, (approximately $70 per month U.S.), the risk reward ratio is very high. Someone has to be desperate for money and willing to risk their life to even consider attempting to bring rare items out of the country.

Within weeks, there was an agreed price of 2,000,000 KPW ($2,200.U.S.), which started the process of obtaining the drawing from the state's secret vaults and smuggling it out of the country.

For someone in the western world, this was not very much money. However, for someone in North Korea, it was a small fortune.

For the sum of 2,000,000 Won, there was the chance opportunity that a family members might be able to be smuggled out of the country. For a few individuals, it was worth the risks.

The exact details were not given ahead of time. The agreement stated that the drawing was to be smuggled into China and would eventually find its way to the offices of the Chen-Lee Tea Company in Hong Kong.

Pyongyang North Korea

Deep in a sub-sub-basement room in the central library of Pyongyang, the capital of North Korea is a series of rooms or halls, where some of the country's bounty in literature is kept.

The Grand People's Study House was built in the 1980's to commemorate Kim Il-sung's 70th birthday. It has over 600 rooms.

Unknown to all but a few, there are collections of works from other places in the world that are kept secret, but to only a few librarians. In this country where freedom and knowledge are controlled by the state, treasures such as these are forbidden from the average person. Even in these hidden rooms, there are rooms where names are recorded if anyone enters looking at something, and other rooms where simply no one is ever allowed in.

On a set schedule, the books and manuscripts were dusted to keep them in pristine condition. These rooms were temperature and humidity controlled.

It was in such a room, where state treasures were kept from the public, that Jung Chang-Sun's childhood friend Duri Sol Ju had enough clearance that allowed him to work in maintaining the state treasures.

Jung Chang-Sun and his friend Duri Sol Ju grew up together. Along with another friend, they attended the state school and studied hard together to get a job that was highly revered. You could always find the three of them together. They had a very tight bond.

One afternoon, without any warning, their friend and his family disappeared. Word had it that one of his relatives had stolen something, and in disgrace, the entire family was picked up by the People's Security police and transported to one of North Korea's famous work camps. It was meant as a show of force to anyone else that was caught stealing. The sentence – life at the camp for the family.

The person caught stealing was simply shot through the head at close range. In some of these cases, the person that was shot got off the easiest. Hard work and torture was the word that came from the camps. Human values were quickly lost, and if someone lived or died, it made little difference to the countries leadership.

North Korea is approximately the size of Pennsylvania with a population of almost 25 million people, which is twice the population of Pennsylvania. The citizens are controlled through militarization, and have been under a dictatorship since World War II.

North Korea is a population that is led by a need for militarization. The result is a strain on the economy resulting in starvation. Without good agriculture and with a corrupt government, life is tough at best.

In comparison, South Korea, which is only two-thirds of the size of North Korea, has nearly double the population and a very thriving economy.

For the people of the north, it is as if they live on a different planet. Current estimates give the number of citizens in work camps/ prisons at about 120,000.

There are approximately 25 of these work camps/ prisons in this small country. Most of their inhabitants are political prisoners and very few ever see the light of freedom again once they have been imprisoned. If picked up for reasons deemed a threat to the state by the State Security police, which is North Korea's "secret police or "Bowibu," North Koreans simply disappear from society.

The camps are known as three-generation camps. It is meant to eliminate any and all resistance to the government policies. Entire families simply disappear as though they never existed. As what happened with Jung Chang-Sun and Duri Sol Ju's childhood friend, whole families are imprisoned.

Occasionally, there are mass executions in public areas. The killings are meant as a reminder to the remaining population that all rules must be followed to the letter.

Except for the mass executions, only rumors come out of the camps as to the horrid conditions. There are no letters or visits by human rights groups.

To the rest of the world, it is hard to imagine these conditions still exist. It is estimated that 400,000 people have died from torture, starvation and execution in the camps.

The disappearance of their friend and his family that day stayed in the memories of the two boys. They pledged that someday, they would find a way out of North Korea. Unfortunately, in this highly controlled state, words come easier than actions. However, in North Korea, even your words might make you a candidate for the next roundup of people.

Years later, Jung Chang-Sun, Duri Sol Ju and their families were still in North Korea. Thoughts of freedom were slowly disappearing from the visions of the North Koreans virtually held captive by the state. With the absolute control of the government, the citizens were not allowed to know that other countries had individual freedoms, including the opportunity to move freely within their countries and to travel to and from their countries. Even the news had been censored.

Both men had a wife and two young boys. They wanted their boys to grow up knowing the taste of freedom.

Jung Chang-Sun came up with the concept. (Even in a highly controlled state like North Korea, there is always a way for a price.) One evening, he and Duri Sol Ju discussed how they could raise enough money to get their families out of North Korea. The desire was still strong in their memories.

It would not be cheap. It would be well beyond the means for most people in North Korea. However, it was possible.

Jung Chang-Sun had worked his plan for years, establishing the connections that might allow him and his family to flee North Korea. Now, in secrecy, he shared with his friend a scheme that he felt had a chance of working.

He knew the secret rooms where his friend Duri Sol Ju worked contained things so secret that no one ever saw them. In fact, except for a log sheet, they did not exist to the rest of the world.

On top of that, most of those that put the items in the vault were long dead.

As a result, it had become a secret treasure for the officials of the government just in case the country dissolved.

His plan was simple, but would come with a huge risk. They would remove several artifacts from the vault, find a way to get them out of the library without notice, and sell them on the black market.

As they discussed the plan, they figured they might need to remove as many as ten objects to get enough money to pay smugglers to get their families out of North Korea.

To accomplish the task, the items needed to be removed one at a time. They would be smuggled out of the country separately, a month or two apart to avoid suspicion.

Jung Chang-Sun had been working for several years as a truck driver. His work took him on a scheduled run to China every couple of weeks to pick up food supplies.

The repeated trips gave him the opportunity he needed to make some connections with the black market.

Now, they realized the risks were high, and along with it was the high cost of the freedom they might be able to purchase. It was worth the chance.

This was the only plan they had conceived of that had a chance of working. It was probably now or never, and they both knew it.

Just in case something went wrong, neither one of them told their families about their plans.

Chapter 15

The Log Sheet

One morning, while doing his routine maintenance cleaning job, Jung Chang-Sun's friend Duri Sol Ju removed the log sheet for a section of the artifacts in one of the secret rooms of the Grand People's Study House.

He took the log sheet home and hand copied the sheet.

On the copy, he omitted two objects – small drawings from the Tang Dynasty.

The next day, he replaced the sheet in the log.

Waiting another day to make sure it had not been noticed, he hid the one drawing in a place he could retrieve it easily. Then, he rolled up the other drawing, carefully putting it in the sleeve of his jacket. As long as he did not bend his arm, his hope was that no one should notice it when he left the building, and hopefully, it would not be missed.

All day long, he had been thinking about his fate. It was a big risk. One mistake, something out of order, and it would be all over.

At the end of the day, he nervously put on his jacket. The drawing had to be in a location that did not give the appearance that anything was different.

As he left the building, the guard instructed him to open his coat to allow building security to check to see that he did not have anything concealed. He was instructed to empty his pockets as well.

It was standard procedure for all employees as they left work. He had done it every day since he started work at the People's Grand Study House.

Now, it was the moment of truth.

The guards were looking for contraband. It had become routine for them. In fact, it was so routine that the guards had become complacent in their job.

As they searched Duri Sol Ju pockets, Duri hoped that his expression hadn't changed and the guards would not notice that he was starting to perspire.

There was a long line of people leaving their jobs, and Duri was relieved that no one noticed how nervous he had become.

He lifted up his arms while the guards searched his pockets. Finding nothing, they waved him on.

The first part of the plan worked. Duri Sol Ju had gotten the drawing out of the library.

He met his friend in a path between housing groups. There, Duri cautiously put the drawing in the hands of his friend Jung Chang-Sun. For the first time that day, he took a deep breath. Now, he knew his friend would be starting to worry about his part of the smuggling.

He wasn't totally in the clear. If Jung Chang-Sun was caught, he might be forced to give up the name of his conspirator.

The next week, Jung Chang-Sun was scheduled to make the run into a border town in China along with three other trucks to pick up food. The trucks looked like 1950's vehicles without anything fancy. Jung's truck had a single axle in back without dual tires. It was your basic covered transport truck.

There was a tiny gap between the truck body and the frame behind the cab. Jung covered the drawing with paper the same color as the truck and attached it to the truck body in the gap. The drawing was well hidden from view by the panels of the truck.

When he reached the border, he was hoping that nothing appeared out of the ordinary.

Security was extremely strict at the border crossing. However, leaving an underdeveloped country such as North Korea, the border agents were not looking for a drawing. They were paying attention to anyone hiding on the truck trying to get out of the country.

Small spaces drew only a glancing look. The guards were more interested in the boxes, along with the undercarriage of the trucks. The armed guards were searching the trucks with extreme care.

As Jung Chang-Sun pulled his truck up to the inspection station, he held his breath. A long red and white striped poll blocked the road. Two stern looking soldiers with Russian AK47s stood at the front of the truck, while two others positioned themselves at the rear. The officer in charge motioned to him that he wanted to look at his paperwork.

His papers were the same as the two trucks before him. As the officer inspected his papers and identification, two more guards did a complete search of the back of the truck. Mirrors were used to check the undercarriage and wheel wells. The officer was looking for changes in drivers or other alterations that might have been made in the orders.

The stop had been exactly the same as the past trips he had taken into China. Jung Chang-Sun was expected to travel fifteen kilometers into China to pick up supplies at a warehouse and return within four hours.

A list of family members was attached to the order sheet. It was intimidation to keep the driver from running.

After a brief inspection, they raised the roadblock and the officer waved him on.

Holding his breath, he watched in his rear-view mirror as the pole came back down blocking the next vehicle in line.

He did it. He got through the border station.

Arriving at his destination, his contact from the black market was there to make the exchange. His contact was working as part of the loading group. Knowing the risk of someone saying something, they were extremely careful to make sure no one was watching.

Things went very smooth.

On the return trip, Jung Chang-Sun hid the money back in the narrow panel of the truck. Even though the truck was searched at the border, since the border guards were used to the trucks making the round trip, they failed to detect the extra cargo.

As he drove back to the transport office, the expression on his face slowly turned from one of concern, to a smile.

One thing crossed his mind. The government would often change drivers on routes that crossed the border to prevent people from planning escapes. As a result, he had no idea how long he would be able to stay in this job.

Along with the drawing, Jung Chang-Sun left a short list of other items with his black market contact that might be available, stating that he and his friend felt they could safely remove them from the vault without detection. His contact told him he would price them out and get back to him with a price they were willing to pay.

Jung Chang-Sun suggested that the price needed to be higher than for the first object. The risks he was taking were too high.

Arriving back in Pyongyang, Jung Chang-Sun did not make contact with Duri Sol Ju. They had decided they needed to be safe. Just in case someone had been suspicious, they would wait two days before making contact again.

Hong Kong

The shipment of the Tang Dynasty drawing was eagerly anticipated by the "organization." Advance word had been received that the goods were out of the country. Bidding was already north of $200,000 U.S. and they had only started talking to their clients the day before, when they were confident that the goods would be delivered.

It was a Wednesday afternoon when a courier arrived at the office of the Chen-Lee Tea Company in Hong Kong. Once again, after the exchange of funds, the manager found himself in possession of a very expensive drawing.

Opening the package, he found a drawing rolled up inside a protective cardboard tube, packed securely in the package with paper scraps. He carefully slid the drawing out of its protective tube.

The drawing was from the 700's A.D. It depicted a scenic drawing along with a well-known Confucian saying written in Chinese script. For something that was over thirteen hundred years old, it was in magnificent shape. Even the colors were still vibrant. It would definitely bring an excellent price on the open market.

So far, the top bid was from a client in Chicago. It was determined that the package would be routed through several locations similar to the way the other shipments were done.

What wasn't expected was that the Chinese government had picked up word of the shipment. Someone had heard about the availability of such a drawing and put things together as to how it was being taken across China. As a result, the joint taskforce on artifact smuggling had been monitoring the shipment from the time it had been spotted, traveling through Central China.

As the team discussed the shipment, the concern was; if they recovered the artifact, who or where would it be properly returned? It appeared that the proper ownership was still in serious question.

In the next week, the package would be tracked from Hong Kong, through Vancouver, and then to Toronto. Valuable information intercepted on the "organization" by Chinese and Canadian intelligence organizations, indicated that they anticipated that the package would be smuggled into the U.S. through Duluth, on the Calvin Wroth. Now, it would be up to Canadian and U.S. Customs officials to put the pieces together on the "organization" regarding how and where the transfers would be made. The offices of ICE and Homeland Security in New Jersey were busy once again.

If it wasn't for a tip from China that a package was in transit, it probably never would have been spotted by Canadian Customs when it arrived in Vancouver. After arriving in Vancouver, without any problems from Customs, the package was safely sent by express shipment to the "organization's" offices in Toronto.

What wasn't seen was a tiny modified RFI wire that could not be picked up with the normal RFI scanner. The RFI wire was similar to what libraries and merchants use to make sure items are not stolen when people leave the buildings. Only this one had been modified using a secret method, for the use by Customs.

Canadian Customs, in Vancouver, had slipped the wire into the packaging when it entered the country, in order to aid in the secret tracking of the package.

Customs figured that the package would probably be modified at each major location along its journey. If they could slip something into the packing, it had a chance of staying with the package. They needed to establish the list of contacts in Toronto and the handlers where it was to exit Canada.

So far, the trick appeared to be working. The RFI wire was working as the package was delivered to an office in Vancouver.

The office and the individuals working there were put on constant surveillance. Nothing went in or out of the area without the detection of Canadian Customs. Cameras and scanners were set up in the elevator and stairs of the building along with cameras on the street covering the exits.

The building's maintenance was modified so that Custom's officers could scan the inside of the office each day checking for the presence of their RFI strip and the package. If the package with the RFI strip moved, they would know it. If the sensor was removed from the package, they would know later that day when they rescanned the office and assume that the package was on the move. Even if anyone left the building with a package during the week, they would have visual evidence of everything and everyone leaving the building. With the cellphone intercepts, the Canadians already had a good idea of the "organization's" next move.

The drawing only stayed in Vancouver one day. From there, the people in the office had changed the outer box to eliminate the Customs lettering and the new box was off to Toronto via express delivery. The RFI wire remained in the stuffing around the drawing.

The package arrived in Toronto and was delivered by the shipping company to a small office the next day. It seemed like a very indirect route for something that valuable, but for security reasons, it kept the "organization" safe from mistakes. It would be nearly impossible to track the shipments back to them.

One had to remember, this was not the only package they had in shipment at any one time.

The surprise for the Customs Agents came on the next leg of the journey. It was hand delivered to a person in Sault Ste. Marie. In breaking the pattern of shipping by carrier, the smugglers actually drove it to the next location.

There, the drawing was given to the wife of a dockworker.

Now, the Canadian Customs agents finally knew how it was going to be put on the ship.

The question was; who would be the person who would take possession on the ship?

Chapter 16

In Transit

The offices of Customs in both the U.S. and Canada were in constant communication that afternoon.

The agencies traced the shipment of the drawing from China to several cities in Canada and now they were anticipating it to be smuggled into the U.S. on an ore carrier. It felt as if they were watching a shell game. The pea was moving from cup to cup; watching at each location to make sure it had not been spotted before arriving at its destination.

It became obvious why the delivery to Sault Ste. Marie had been done by personal car. With the schedule of the ship, the smugglers could not afford to have the package arrive even an hour after they loaded. They needed to be sure it was at the dock at the right time.

Now, the questions were starting to mount. Should law enforcement officers follow the package all the way to the buyer? Where and when would they intercept it? Who were the contacts on the ore boat and in Duluth?

They still had two deaths to investigate. So far, they were not making very good progress on them.

At the same time, they were still working on a strategy for how they were planning to take down the entire "organization" at one time. Timing and planning was essential.

Stubby O'Shea on the Calvin Wroth

The Calvin Wroth was on its last leg of the scheduled shipments of iron ore from Two Harbors to Sault Ste. Marie. Once they unloaded, they would receive their new orders for shipments, which would probably be out of the Duluth harbor. It was getting late in the year. The shipping season would be over soon.

The Calvin Wroth was loaded down with ore and as they cleared the breakwater heading for open water, Swede and I started our job of tying down the covers for the holds. It was a sunny day. However, there was definitely a cool bite to the wind on that day.

Two hours later, we were tired and ready for something hot to eat. That was the one thing I was enjoying about being on the ship, the hot food was good and available when we were done with our jobs.

As we headed down to the mess, we spotted the new 3rd Mate posting a message on the board. As we got closer, the 3rd Mate turned to us and said, "Storms a comin'. Make sure you got everything tied up topside."

It was not what we were expecting to hear. I was hoping that he was posting the new schedule for our trip from Sault Ste. Marie to Duluth. Now, Swede and I just looked at each other. Storm? How bad? Well, either way we needed to head back up topside and make sure everything was tied down and in a position that would not move in a storm. The temperature was already dropping. Any storm now could bring snow or even worse – ice on the decks.

Our warm meal would have to wait. It was time for one last double check of the decks. No one wanted to be topside in the middle of a snowstorm, or when ice was forming on the decks. We put our heavy jackets back on and headed up.

By the time we got the walk-around finished, I could see the leading edge of the clouds forming to the west. We headed back down to see if there were any further bulletins on the storm.

Sure enough, there was an update. It was a full gale warning. Strong winds followed by freezing temperatures. The good thing; it looked as though we were only going to get a few inches of snow.

Turning back to Swede, I commented that I was glad they were only predicting a few inches of snow.

"That's not the problem," he informed me quite emphatically. "With that wind and temperature, we could get four or five inches of ice up on the deck. I'll give you one guess whose job it will be to chip that away from the holds to get them open at Sault Ste. Marie. It's going to take a few hours."

I thought about it for a few seconds. I really didn't like the thought of chipping ice out on a cold windy deck. Now, I realized why the pay was so good on the ships. Without it, no one would sign up to do the work.

"Well, let's get some warm food and rest before we have to get up early tomorrow to chip ice," I told Swede.

"Remember the last storm? I suggested that you consider missing a meal. Well, this one may show you why," he warned me.

I just stared at him. I was hoping we would reach the end of the shipping season without hitting the "big one." The look on

Swede's face told me that he was expecting something a lot worse than the last storm.

"Think the captain will turn her back and stay in port until it passes?" I foolishly asked.

"Nope! You had better take a couple of those pills you said you had on board. Let's get some rest while we can."

Agent Mark Lawson

I got a phone call from both my FBI contacts in New Jersey and their ICE agents. I guess they felt I needed a little heads up for a change that something was about to happen.

They informed me that there was a package that was about to be shipped from Canada to Duluth on the Calvin Wroth. They had been trying to monitor phone numbers, and they gave me the contact names in Toronto and in Sault Ste. Marie that they knew were involved in the smuggling.

I thanked them for the heads up. With this information, I was hoping that there might be phone calls from either location to one of the burner phones that were used in the past. If they turned the cell phones on, anticipating a call, we might be able to get a location. With any luck, there might be a patrol car within a few blocks that could spot a car or person without being seen.

It was the type of mistake I was hoping someone might do. So far, all our other attempts to find links to the killers had fallen through. Deputy Alex North's attempt to pick up any stray gossip from Two Harbors had also drawn a blank. She informed me that the ore terminal in Two Harbors would be shutting down for the winter season shortly. This looked as though it was our best shot, and perhaps our only one, at finding a link.

I thanked my fellow agents from New Jersey for their heads up. It was encouraging to see them using the system as it was meant to be used.

It was only a half hour later that I received a message from one of my agents. The burner phone in Duluth had been turned on. It looked like someone was expecting to make, or receive a call. Our agent in Duluth was informed of the situation and we had the location being traced.

A few minutes later, we had a location. It was at a warehouse in Superior, Wisconsin. It was just across the high John A. Blatnik into Wisconsin from Duluth. Surveillance was quickly set up for the location.

From what we could see from a first glance, it did not look as though the warehouse was very active. It was an older warehouse with only two cars in the parking lot. I sent another agent up to Duluth to work with our agent assigned to the port city. In the meanwhile, I had the police chief in Superior give me a heads up on the location, including what they knew about it. According to their records, it was a small tool distributor with only a couple employees.

About an hour later, there was a phone call to the burner phone. It was a short call that lasted only five minutes. The call had been made from another burner phone, which we located in Toronto.

When the call was done, the phone was once again shut down by removing the battery. Canadian teams were attempting to locate the source of the cell phone call.

The Canadian location turned out to be a large office building. It would be hard to track it down to an individual or even an office area.

On a hunch, I had my team look at the cell tower records to see if there had been a call placed to and from our locations within an hour prior to the call made on the burner phones. For once, we had a hit. It indicated that there had been a very short cell message.

Now we finally had a link to some possible names and addresses attached to two of the burner phones that we could pursue.

Chapter 17

The "Big" One

Stubby O'Shea on the Calvin Wroth

The prediction of the impending storm turned out to be accurate. The low, dark bank of storm clouds I saw from up on deck, was the leading edge of a strong late-November gale. It hit us about three hours after we secured the deck.

The ship was tossed about like a stick floating in the breaking waves. With the storm, the temperature had suddenly dropped to below freezing, even though the surface water temperature was still a warm thirty-nine degrees.

Unfortunately, it was the spray from the waves that coated the cold deck of the ship. It was forming a solid coating of ice on everything it touched.

Now, as I lay in my bunk, trying hard not to get seasick, I realized that not only had I missed dinner, but now I would have to get up early to report on deck.

We would be in port by two o'clock in the afternoon. If it normally took almost two hours to unfasten the hold covers, I had no idea how long it would take to break them free from the icy grip provided by the storm. The holds would probably be frozen down.

That meant I would have only one chance to eat in the twenty-four hours period. That was breakfast tomorrow morning, provided my stomach could make it through the night. So far, my head felt a little light, but I was handling things.

Unlike the great thunderstorms we had encountered in the past, this storm was silent with the exception of the howling wind that swept the decks. The booming thunder in the holds, caused by the thunderstorms, was replaced by the eerie sound of ice building up and cracking up on the superstructure.

As the ship's hull bent ever so slightly with the large waves, massive sheets of ice on deck cracked and reformed constantly. To a rookie, like myself, the cracks and groans, echoing down the ship, made it sound like the ship was breaking apart all night long.

I was starting to wonder if the person I replaced had indeed had a vision. Perhaps we were all doomed just like the Edmond Fitzgerald. How much weight would six inches of ice covering the deck weigh? Would we make the journey only to hit bottom trying to enter the harbor? How long did it take for the Edmond Fitzgerald to sink?

It was a very long night, with very little sleep.

About five bells, I heard a loud knocking on my cabin door. It was Swede.

"Come-on. Time to get up. Let's get some food in our guts before we need to head topside," he bellowed at me.

Looking at the clock, I must have fallen asleep for at least....well, maybe fifteen minutes. I'm sure it was longer, but honestly, it felt like fifteen minutes.

I shuffled over and put on my warm clothes. Then, I joined him in the corridor before heading to the mess.

The sun was still a couple of hours from rising, but we decided to check out one of the side portholes to see what it looked like outside. The ships lights lit up the rails like something out of Disney's snow castles.

Ice was hanging all over the rails. It looked like it was about four inches thick. I was sure the porthole forward would have been totally covered with ice from the spray all night.

"I've seen worse," Swede exclaimed. "Let's get some warm chow in us before we have to hit the deck. It's going to be a long morning."

"It's still dark. We're going to hit the deck before sunrise?" I asked.

"Ain't you heard of lights," came the disgusted sounding answer. "Let's eat."

I followed him to the mess. When we got there, all the rest of the deck hands were already sitting at the tables.

"Stubby, did you make it through the night?"

I looked up and saw Eric with a big grin. He was waiting for me to inform him that I was too sick to eat.

"No sweat," I replied. "Only, now I'm so hungry I could even eat your cookin."

Eric smiled. He knew I was jawing with him. He gave me a full plate of ham and eggs.

"Thanks," I told him.

When we sat down, I asked Swede, one more time, why we needed to get up so early.

He answered, "Well, we won't go topside until first light. This might be the only meal you get until dinner today. So, you better enjoy it, and let it settle in your gut before breakin ice. That's what the rest of us are doing. At first light, we will all be up on deck breakin ice until our backs get sore.

"There's another reason we get up early. It is to be totally awake before hitting the deck. We don't need anyone half-awake making a mistake and slipping off into the water.

"It's going to be headbusters and safety lines topside this morning. Half of the crew will start from the bow and the rest of us from the stern. We have to get the holds freed by eleven bells. If we get done early, we'll knock the ice off any of the railings that might still be coated. We want things free of ice before we hit port and have to start unloading."

"You think we can do all of it by eleven bells?" I asked.

"I got a ten spot we finish by ten," he told me as he shoveled in another bite of food.

When we were finished eating, and discussing what was needed, we moved out of the mess area and picked up the headbusters.

Now, coming from Jersey, I had a good idea what they were talkin about. When there was trouble on the docks, the headbusters appeared from no-where. Back in my high school days, I thought they were called baseball bats. I learned.

Each of us were given four bats to start with. "Why four?" I asked.

"Haven't you ever broken one of these?" Swede asked. "We use wood so we don't damage anything important, like locks and railings. One storm, I think I broke nine of them busting loose the ice. That was a bad one.

I just stared at him.

"This one's not that bad. You'll see."

"Isn't there a way we could have pre-treated the area, or put salt on the deck?" I persisted.

"To be honest, none of them work very well. You can pre-treat with a spray. However, the deck gets real slippery when you try to spray anything on it. And, with the spray of water from the ship, you have to keep doing it. It's probably more dangerous being on deck spraying it than working on the built-up ice later.

"As for salt, it will just wash off the ship as well. The part that doesn't will speed up the rust. Then, you have to get out and scrape it and repaint the areas even more than we do now.

"Naw! For this temperature, this is the best solution. If it were colder, the ship would have probably found a quiet port to ride this storm out.

"Now, if we were empty, the Captain would have turned her back. He doesn't like his ships getting top heavy."

About seven bells, the order was given to hit the deck. When we forced open the door to the main deck, it was a mass of ice and water. The sky was still as menacing looking dark as it could be from the clouds surrounding the ship.

As instructed, we fastened our safety chains to the rail after swatting it once or twice with the bat to knock the ice off. Then, we started on the first hold.

After a couple mighty home-run swings, I realized that I didn't need to swing the headbusters that hard. It was a good thing. If I did, I would have been wiped out before I got to the fourth hold.

As it turned out, the holds were still warm. All that ore in the holds, along with the ship sitting deep in the water, kept the holds warm all night. The heat rising from the warm hold was helping us melt the ice from the bottom side. With a quick swat, large chunks of ice broke off and were pushed to the side with each swing.

It didn't take long before I started to realize that the low dark clouds were actually fog. The warm water was causing the mist to form a cloud over the water, which had turned into a cloud in the cooler air high above. Before long, the sun warmed the clouds, and the fog started to burn off, giving us a helping hand in melting the ice.

Even the light breeze was helping us. The air in the layer just above the lake was still holding at 39 degrees, thanks to the water temperature. As I watched, once the sun hit the railings, I saw large pieces of ice falling off the ship, like snow falling off the limbs of a tree.

I started to feel better. It was not going to be a back-breakin morning of slamming ice. It was more like chipping it up into reasonable size pieces and pushing the large chunks overboard.

Swede won the bet. We were done by ten bells. We had an hour to clean up, put on some dry clothes, and be ready to start unlashing the holds before we made port. If someone had asked me earlier this morning if we would be ready, I would have said no-way.

By the time we were in sight of port, in Sault Ste. Marie, almost all the ice was off the ship. To someone on shore, they would have thought it was just another transit across the big lake.

At one o'clock, we were nuzzling up to the terminal – right on schedule. They tied her off to the dock and commenced the unloading procedure. As we did, I paid attention to the loud noise the conveyor made hauling the ore off the dock. Compared to eight seamen with clubs beating ice, I wasn't sure which was the loudest.

My ears were still ringing from all the noise we made earlier. I wished I had put earplugs in before we started beating on the holds. If someone had a sound meter, I'll bet we were louder than the noise from a thunderstorm. Who needed a ships horn. Just put eight of us on deck with bats.

Somehow, I wondered if there had been any rats onboard. If there was, my guess was that they were still looking for a place to hide.

It felt good to be on a more relaxed tempo for unloading and restocking the ship. It had been a long morning after not getting any sleep. At least I didn't get seasick. That would have been the worst.

We were about three-fourths the way finished with our unloading when I heard a small crash on the dock. One of the fork truck operators that was moving supplies for the ship, had inadvertently knocked a metal container off the top of a pallet.

Glancing over at the commotion, out of the side of my eye, I accidentally spotted something else. Someone was placing a small box on top of a railroad tie near the rear gangway.

I used my cell phone to get his photo.

Within a minute, one of our crew calmly walked down, picked it up, and bought it onboard. He was looking around to see if anyone was watching. Fortunately, I was partially obscured by the winch I was greasing. I got a weak photo of him with the package.

I figured I would get a chance later on to get a better shot of him somewhere on the ship.

I recognized the crewmember with the package. It was one of our electronic engineers. Paul Radcliff had been one of the quiet engineers onboard that I had only limited contact with since being on the ship. I had seen him in the mess and occasionally in the fitness room. However, he always kept to himself and I figured that was just his personality.

I was trying to figure out how I could leave my station and follow him, to see where he put the package. In an 855-foot long vessel, there are many places someone could put something down and no one would be the wiser.

I lost him when he stepped back into the superstructure.

As I kept a watch of the activities on the dock, I started to think about how easy it was for Radcliff to slip down the gangway and pick up a package. Everyone else on deck was watching the sloppy fork truck driver.

That was when it hit me. What if the accident in Two Harbors was really an accident? What if that bucket was meant to be a distraction and not actually hit someone? I know I would have been shouting at the worker, using some rather strong language. I'm guessing Blacky knew some words as well from working below deck all these years. Could it have been a diversion to draw attention, while something was taken off the ship? If it was, I missed it, and so did everyone else.

It was just a hunch. However, I got my cell phone out and sent a message to my boss in Jersey.

"Package picked up in Sault Ste. Marie. Electronics Engineer Paul Radcliff picked it up when fork truck driver caused a diversion on dock. Send photo of Radcliff later. Was Two Harbors part of a diversion as well??? - Stubby"

I attached the photos I had just taken and copied Agent Mark Lawson on the note as well. This might change the way we looked into the killing. The important thing, I let them know that Radcliff picked up the package. Now that it was onboard, we could be ready for them at our next stop in Duluth.

I could send them a photo of Paul Radcliff later when he was in a position where he wouldn't realize that I took his picture. Working out in the fitness room would give me an excuse to take pictures of the equipment, and hopefully Radcliff.

We finished loading our supplies and left port right on schedule. With the big storm last night, I would have guessed that we would have been at least six hours behind schedule. At least for now, the sun was shining and the lake had calmed down. We looked good for making port in Duluth by late morning tomorrow.

During the trip, I managed to get a better picture of Electronics' Engineer Paul Radcliff using my cell phone, when he was working out after dinner. Unfortunately, I still had no idea where he had stashed the package he picked up in the last port. It was a big ship, and so far, the scanner the Canadians had supplied me had not picked up any trace of the telltale wire. With all the metal in the superstructure of the ship, it was probably well shielded.

Chapter 18

Arrival

Agent Mark Lawson

I hadn't even seen my text message from Stubby, when a phone call from the ICE and FBI Agents In-Charge in New Jersey came in.

"Mark, this is Agent Kyle Easton from ICE and Agent Roy Hacket from New Jersey FBI. Did you see the note from Stubby on the Calvin Wroth? We figured we should get all of us on the line to discuss our next moves.

"We tried getting ahold of Customs Agent Olson in Minneapolis, but he was in a meeting."

I had turned the volume of the cell phone down when I had an important meeting in my office. They had just left, and I was just turning the volume back on when the phone had rung.

The cell phone showed that I had missed two messages during our meeting.

"No, fill me in," I told them.

They filled me in on Stubby's message, while I reviewed on my phone what the message actually said.

"Well, a possible diversion brings another look to the Two Harbor's case doesn't it," I suggested. "Maybe they are not as smart as we thought they were, and don't know we have Stubby on board."

"That was my thought as well," Agent Easton informed me. "I'm not going to tell Stubby that though. He's safer thinking someone might be on to him and stay alert.

"The reason we called you was to request that you monitor the burner phones numbers you identified earlier. See if there is any chance someone received a call or text, from either Toronto or Sault Ste. Marie today, letting them know the package is onboard the Calvin Wroth," Agent Easton told me.

"Our guess is that someone will be waiting for it in Duluth. We'll have Agent Olson try and pick him up on surveillance. You might want to touch base with him and see if his group needs any assistance."

"Sounds like a plan," I conferred. I was assuming that they wanted me to keep a close "out of the way" distance. Since they opened the door to my talking to Agent Olson, it would give me an excuse to get more information out of him as well.

I sent a note to one of our agents here in Minneapolis to put a net around phone calls between Sault St. Marie, Toronto and Duluth. Watch especially close for our burner phone numbers plus the cell phone numbers we picked up from the last communications.

The boat, oops I meant ship, isn't due in port until tomorrow. However, it was time to start monitoring, and I set the initial time period for the monitoring of the cell phone coverage to an hour before Stubby's last message. By checking for cell tower traffic between those cities, we hoped to find some links.

I knew I could get it approved quickly by a judge.

I decided to give Deputy Alex North a call, and fill her in on the new information.

When I called Alex, I caught her while she was writing a ticket on some county road. She told me that she would call me back as soon as she was free. She hinted that I wouldn't believe this one.

As I was waiting for her to call back, I just sat there wondering, *"Where was my mind that I didn't even think about asking where everyone was on the ship when the accident happened, and if anyone saw someone in a place they normally wouldn't have been."* Dumb rookie mistake!

About thirty minutes later, Deputy Alex North called me back.

"Well Agent Lawson, did you just realize that you missed the deer season. When are you planning on heading north?"

I laughed. "Thanks. It's been busy enough down here. So what was your big bust you were working on?"

"You won't believe this; I had to write a ticket to an eighty-five year old man that was driving a riding mower down the wrong side of the road. Apparently, he was going to visit a friend down the road.

"Someone complained that they came over a hill and almost hit the man. He was almost in the middle of the gravel road. They had to swerve and almost went off the road. They called in the complaint.

"I figured by writing the ticket, his family would have to take him to see the judge. Knowing how our judge works, he'll get the family to agree to keep him off the road with the mower and throw out the ticket."

"Well Deputy, you get the best cases.

"I thought you might like to know, I got a message from Stubby O'Shea this morning.

"He said they used a diversion this morning, to sneak a package onboard the Calvin Wroth. The ship's heading for Duluth. We were all wondering if we lost something in our investigation.

"Do you think Brasso's death might have been an accident, when they were trying to create a diversion? What if Stubby wasn't the target?" I asked her. "We were looking for a way that they would have known who was leaving the ship, so they could set it up. What if that part of the equation didn't matter? It would make it simpler if it was just a real accident."

"You're right, Alex replied. "We were looking at only one possibility. We never did map out everyone that was on the dock or ship.

"So, you think there was a drop in Two Harbors?"

"It is a definite possibility. We may never know. Keep a low profile. Our first guess may have still been the correct one."

Before we hung up, I told her I would buy her lunch the next time I was in her territory. It had been enjoyable working with her.

I finally got a call back from Agent Olson.

After a short discussion with him, Agent Olson revealed a little more about what Customs expected to happen in Duluth when the ship pulled in.

Olson thanked me for agreeing to once again monitor the cell signals.

I decided that I would drive up to Duluth to be there when the Calvin Wroth arrived. It was definitely ICE's case. However, with an extra set of eyes watching everyone else, I might come in handy, especially if they ran another diversion. This case was only growing in strength.

The Calvin Wroth was due to pick up a load of coal, and haul it back east. To assist in the surveillance, I decided to find a spot on the top of one of the nearby grain terminals and use a spotting scope to watch everything that was going on. Our FBI spotting scope had a camera mount on it. As a result, if I detected anything, I could take a quick photo of the action.

The next day, I was all set up to start our surveillance.

So far, the ship was right on schedule. The Duluth Shipping Times had listed it correctly, including listing of the dock where the ship was expected to load.

It was a pleasant sunny day when I spotted the Calvin Wroth out on the open water, heading for the ship channel that led from Lake Superior to the harbor.

Passing under the lift bridge, it gave the customary horn signal as it was about to enter the harbor.

Chapter 19

Concerns

Pyongyang North Korea

With the first Tang Dynasty drawing delivered to the contact in China, and money in their hands, it was time for Jung Chang-Sun and Duri Sol Ju to plan their second theft.

Even though Jung Chang-Sun had left a short list of possible items that were available with his contact in China, Duri Sol Ju had already removed the second drawing off the log.

It would be the next to go. They would attempt to remove it from the room the same way they had done with the first drawing.

As Jung Chang Sun was thinking about the shipping schedule for smuggling out their second drawing in his truck on its run to China, he overheard a conversation with some of the workers at the warehouse that disturbed him.

It started out as one of those "heard on the street" rumors. However, very soon it was obvious that there was a level of credibility with the report.

One of the warehouse workers was telling a group of his co-workers that his cousin's boy was picked up by the secret police – the Bowibu.

The story began with a boy that did not like to follow directions. His parents were always looking for him. Whenever the boy told them he would stay close by, he would wander past the boundaries his parents had set.

This concerned his parents. They did not want the People's Security police to come to their door telling them their son was being arrested as well as the rest of the family for being associated with the wrong kind of people.

According to what Jung Chang-Sun heard at the warehouse, the boy had taken a walk to go to the market. That was where the story got fuzzy, the co-worker said.

Whether he made it to the market or took a detour earlier, somehow he ended up near one of the North Korea prison camps.

He had been forbidden by his parents to go anywhere near the prison camp.

On this day, the North Korean government was planning one of their demonstrations meant to keep the North Korean people in line. Several of the prisoners were going to be executed in the plaza in front of the prison.

As the boy approached the plaza, a crowd had assembled. The boy's curiosity brought him to join the crowd to see what was happening.

As people gathered all around the boy, he heard people say that there was going to be a demonstration.

At the time, he did not understand the seriousness of the situation. He did not know to what extent a demonstration by the military was about.

Soon, he saw military people gathering in front of the camp as well as on the sides of the crowd that gathered outside. They were heavily armed as they usually were in public.

After a few minutes, five prisoners were brought out in chains. They were lined up in front of the crowd.

A military man gave the crowd a speech about respecting the wishes of their Supreme Chairman, and not speaking out of line. All of the prisoners were political prisoners, and they were here to show everyone what happens to those who do not follow their leader.

After the speech, five of the military men who had escorted the prisoners from the prison walked up to the prisoners who were now on their knees in front of the crowd.

There was a buzz in the crowd. Within a minute, the command was given to shoot.

With pistols drawn, all five men were shot in the back of their heads. They fell on their faces directly in front of the crowd.

The boy panicked after seeing the execution. Pinned in by the crowd, he forced his way out of the crowd pushing his way to the back.

The military men on the side of the crowd tried to stop him. They wanted the crowd to stay where they were until the bodies were carried away. However, all the boy had in mind was fleeing the scene.

As he fled, he almost knocked down several men. Unknown to the others, they were members of the Bowibu.

That afternoon, the police tried in vain to find the boy. They wanted to reprimand both him and his family.

Word got back to the boy's family, informing them that their son was at the execution in the plaza, and that he was seen running from the area

.

According to the person telling the story in the warehouse, the family was so frightened they hid the boy and forbid him from going outside for the next two weeks. They wanted to make sure none of the police recognized him.

Even with keeping the boy inside, later that day, the People's Security police knocked at their door.

The police demanded to know why the boy was at the execution. Who did they know that was there?

When it was over, they took the boy in for additional questioning. They were still looking to find out if the family had any ties to any of the prisoners.

The family was lucky; it could have been the Bowibu knocking at the door.

For Jung Chang-Sun, it was another example of why they needed to get their families out of North Korea, quickly. The family of the boy was lucky that he had not been caught at the demonstration and the family thrown into a camp. People had been thrown in camps for lesser offenses.

For Jung Chang-Sun and Duri Sol Ju it was a big concern. Soon, their sons would be old enough to want to test the North Korean restrictions.

With the shipping schedule set in place for a trip to China for food, Jung Chang-Sun realized that his friend Duri's calmness was also starting to erode.

They had gotten away with the first caper. Were they really that lucky that they could get away with removing enough items to pay for a safe transit for their families out of North Korea? Even if they were successful, where would they go?

They wouldn't have passports or a visa. What if another country stopped them and sent them back to North Korea? What would happen to them then?

Duri Sol Ju's mind was racing as well the entire night filled with "what if's," and they needed to smuggle out another drawing the next day.

As the sun rose, Duri Sol Ju put on his heavy jacket before walking to work.

He had a usual route that he took every day when he walked to and from work. On this day, all the way to the Grand People's Study House, he was watching to see if anyone was paying attention to him. Surely, he thought, someone must know what they were doing. Even the walls seemed to have ears.

As he dusted and re-cataloged the artwork on the list for today's cleaning, he kept thinking about the procedure he would follow as he left work. Internally, his tension was rising. He would only have one chance to do it right.

At the end of his workday, Duri Sol Ju calmly walked over to the spot in the massive room where he had hidden the second drawing. He slid it carefully into his long coat sleeve, making sure there was nothing to indicate anything was inside his coat.

"So far so good," he thought. *"Now as I leave the room I need to look around to see if anyone is watching me."*

Making his way up the many flights of steps to the first security station, on the level below the library floors, Duri Sol Ju was joined by a few other workers. They were from other locations in the building. At the last flight of stairs, where two stairways met and led to the security area, they greeted him as several workers continued up the stairs.

Reaching the security station, Duri Sol Ju started to realize, *"Well, if I get caught, everyone will know what happened. I'll bet the guards will change their methods of watching their workers."*

It was a sobering thought. The part he left out was whether the Bowibu would shoot him on the spot in front of the others, or give him a mock trial first.

The two guards used the same procedure they did every day. Nothing had changed.

They checked everyone's pockets to make sure nothing was in their coats. They didn't even make them take them off prior to checking. That was their flaw; repetitive procedures by an authority gave them no power to deviate from a written procedure. Everyone was simply following orders as given.

One by one, the workers in line went through security. There were no smiles or cordial conversations to the guards. Everything was by the book.

With a large feeling of relief, Duri Sol Ju exited the building, just as the sun was setting, and took a breath of freedom. Once again, he had beaten the system. He looked for someone watching him as he walked.

Unfortunately, his confidence of being able to continue the thefts was diminishing by the minute. Every time he saw anyone looking his way, his nervousness increased.

Later that evening, when Duri Sol Ju met Jung Chang-Sun, he handed the drawing over to him, and quietly told him, "We were lucky my friend. I'm not sure if our luck will hold out much longer. You realize, it will only take one slip. Maybe we should quit and find another way to exit the country."

Jung Chang-Sun took the drawing from Duri Sol Ju.

"Have faith. Only a few more artifacts and we can talk to some people about getting over the border."

"How?" Duri Sol Ju asked. "Who can we safely ask?"

Jung Chang-Sun shrugged. "They'll know how," he answered. "My contacts have friends. They'll find a way, just have faith."

To Duri Sol Ju, it was not as reassuring as he hoped.

Later that week, when supplies were to be picked up in China, Jung Chang-Sun delivered the drawing to his contacts at the warehouse in China.

Once again, the formalities were the same at the border crossing, and the small drawing was well hidden in the small area between the truck's cab and the baggage area.

When Jung Chang-Sun met his contact, he was paid 2,500,000 Won ($2,750 U.S.) for the drawing. To Jung Chang-

Sun, it felt as though he had made a great bargaining agreement. His demand for an increased price had been met.

Chapter 20

Duluth Harbor

Agent Mark Lawson - Duluth, Minnesota

It was almost 11:30 am, by the time the big cargo ship Calvin Wroth squared off with the coal terminal, and started to move in to tie off its lines to the loading dock in the Duluth harbor.

Actually, the Superior Midwest Energy Terminal was located on the Superior, Wisconsin side of the channel. It had a good space for ships up to 1200 feet long to dock.

I had perched myself on the top of the General Mills grain elevator a short distance away. From here, I had a good, unobstructed view of the coal dock, and at the same time, unless someone had a good pair of binoculars, it would be hard to spot me high above them. With only an empty ship channel between the ship and myself, I could observe all the activities easily.

Between the grain terminals and the steeples of the many churches in both Duluth and Superior, they offered the best perch to observe things on the ground.

Personally, I'd rather be up on the grain terminal than clinging to one of the tall church steeples in town. I was never a lover of heights, and watching the steeplejacks repairing the shingles on the church steeples reminded me why I chose a ground-based job.

That said; even standing on a flat surface, I kept my distance from the edge of the roof. Using a tripod, I had a stable, and thank goodness, an unwavering view. The good thing, since I was back from the edge, it made it harder for anyone on the ground to spot me.

As I scanned the loading dock, I spotted Customs Agent Olson parked in a dark colored pickup near the end of the coal dock. From his location, he had a good view of any activity on the dock. I gave him credit; using a pickup made him seem like any other Wisconsin dockworker.

My guess was that he was probably going to let the regular agents of the Coast Guard board the ship, and go over the manifest and list of those onboard. To someone on the ship, it would appear as though it was business as normal.

The ship was using its thrusters to gently move next to the dock. I watched as the long shoremen caught the ropes and snugged the long vessel to the dock.

I began scanning the ship for any signs of Stubby, or the ship's Electronics Engineer Paul Radcliff. The photo Stubby sent us would help identify Radcliff if he tried to get off the ship.

As I did, I realized the weakness of my location. The spotting scope was extremely powerful and had image stabilization. Therefore, it was like watching a mini-television. Unfortunately, to zoom in far enough to see someone's face, it narrowed my field of view. I had to be careful that I was not watching the gangplank area only to miss someone coming out of a near water-level door, which was designed for allowing regional pilots to board the ship prior to entering the harbor.

As a result, I was constantly zooming in and out.

Remembering what happened in Sault Ste. Marie, I sent a text message to Agent Olson, reminding him to keep a close eye open for a diversion meant to steer his attention away from the real action.

He responded quickly, "Thanks. Hope you tied down your hat up there."

He was right. Even a small breeze on the ground would feel like a hurricane to me at this height. Fortunately, the elevator was built strong, and it was not apt to sway in the wind.

We kept a close watch on the ship as the normal activities of a newly docked ship progressed.

It would have been helpful to use our communication radios. However, since this group seemed to stay one-step ahead of us, we decided yesterday not to use our radios. A skilled group could be listening in to a scanner, and pick up the fact that we were keeping the ship under surveillance.

About a half an hour later, after watching the activities along the dock, I observed a supply truck pull up to the ship. As it did, I noticed a puff of smoke come from its exhaust. It looked from here as though the engine had backfired.

With the puff of smoke, a couple shore workers came running to see what the problem was. The last thing they wanted was to have a truck with engine problems blocking their dock. They had a schedule to meet.

I called Agent Olson on his cell. "What do you think? Looks like a diversion from here."

He agreed. "You watch the stern. I'll watch the bow. If they are going to remove something, this might be their chance."

As my scope swept the stern half of the ship, I spotted Stubby O'Shea. I had spotted him earlier at his stern winch station when the ship came in. Now, he was one hundred feet up from the stern, standing on one of the passageways located on the side of the ship.

Zoomed in on him, I could see he was holding on to the railing. When I looked closer, I realized that he was using his arm to point to someone that was another hundred feet down the ship. His arm was resting on the railing with his finger pointed down the ship. I made a quick scan.

There he was, a man in a dark, reddish hoodie. Until I spotted Stubby, I had missed the seaman as he blended in well with the color of the ship.

Quickly, I notified Agent Olson about the man on deck.

I couldn't get a good look at his face, but obviously, Stubby was keeping him in his view without being too obvious. I wished I had a way of letting him know that we had him in sight as well.

I checked with Agent Olson to see if he had an ID on the seaman. So far, he hadn't seen a good view of the man's face either.

As he reached the bow, he ducked back inside the ship. Now, both of us were watching for him to reappear.

Agent Olson attempted to flash his headlights in an effort to let Stubby know that we had marked his person. We couldn't tell if he saw the signal or not. Stubby was heading towards the same hatch the man had entered. Fortunately, he was a long ways behind him.

I wondered, *"Would the man see him and get spooked? Worse yet, what was Stubby walking into?"*

Now, we were scanning the whole ship looking for signs of either man. So far, we could not see any sign of them. There were sea-doors open in the bow as well as the stern for loading and for ventilation, along with gangways from the top deck located at both ends.

Where were they?

The conveyors were starting to load the coal into the holds. I could hear them all the way over at the grain elevator.

I spotted a tow truck. It was heading for the dock to assist the supply vendor.

If something was going to happen, this was the time.

As it approached the supply truck, I noticed a man with an orange vest leaving the bow service door. His dress was different, but, his face matched the photo Stubby had supplied us.

"Olson, man at the bow service door in the safety vest."

"Got him." the reply came back.

Getting a close-up scan of him, I noticed that he had a small cardboard tube under his arm. I shot a few photos of the man, along with the tube, as I kept him in view. At the same time, I kept reminding myself of what I told Agent Olson – watch for a diversion.

As we watched the man walk over to the tow truck, we saw him put the cardboard tube in the cab of the tow truck.

Then, he headed for the hatch at the rear of the ship.

So far, there was no sign of Stubby. Where had he gone and what happened to him? Agent Olson and I were both wondering the same thing.

As the tow truck got the motor going on the supply truck, I watched it start to drive away from the ship. Then, I heard Agent Olson on my cell phone, "Mark, I'm following the truck."

From my perch, I watched as he pulled out and followed the truck from a good distance.

I was still concerned that we had not seen any sign of Stubby. What happened to him? Did someone blindside him and leave him in a supply room?

I expected him to pop up on deck and point to the man that had deposited the tube in the truck.

As I watched, I decided that someone had to make a safety check, if he didn't show up at the stern winch before the ship sailed. The ship had been loading for almost an hour so far.

Another sixty minutes clicked by. In another hour, the boat would be close to loaded. From my perch on top the elevator, I was starting to get nervous. Something was wrong. I checked with Agent Olson.

"Olson, are you still on the truck?" I asked.

"Yes. He went to a storage yard on Highway #35. No movement so far. I'm about a half a block away. The tube is still in the cab."

"I have a concern here. No sign of Stubby, so far, and the ship is almost loaded. We need to have the Coast Guard find a reason to board the ship prior to its leaving to make sure Stubby is okay if he doesn't show at his winch station," I told him.

"Agreed. Can you set it up?" he asked.

"Done," I responded.

"Hold on a minute," I told him.

I spotted someone in the stern door that appeared to be carrying a few boxes. He was dressed like one of the longshoremen.

In-between two of the boxes I could just make out the end of a tube. As I zoomed into his face, it was Radcliff. This was his third change of clothes since they docked. As I watched, he handed the packages off to someone on the dock.

I shot photos of the action.

"Olson, I think there are two vehicles we need to follow. I gave him the description of the new vehicle. As I finished, I quickly called my FBI agent that was nearby, and gave him the description of the vehicle to tail.

"Don't let them see you and don't lose them," I instructed our agent.

Not to be caught a third time, I kept my surveillance of the ship. There was still the open question of Stubby. I had seen him tail the man into the ship and disappear. Where the heck was he?

It would only take fifteen or twenty minutes before they were done loading and the ship was ready to set sail. Already, I saw signs that the massive engines were being prepared for the voyage.

Smoke was slowly appearing out of the exhaust stacks.

I was just about to call the Coast Guard and ask them to delay the sailing, when I spotted Stubby on the stern winch station. He was standing there with his arms out – but crossed. What did that mean? Was he sending me a signal?

I watched him and scanned the ship as rapidly as I could.

Finally, just before they untied the massive ropes from the dock, I spotted Stubby pointing to the stern ramp. There, what appeared to be an employee of the Coast Guard, was a man coming down the ramp with what appeared to be a clipboard.

When I checked closer, there was something under his arm as well. It was a tube. Who was this person? Was he really with the Coast Guard?

Realizing that we were under orders not to trust anyone and to keep other agencies out of the investigation, I put in a quick call to Rick Bernaski, the Douglas County Sheriff, whom I had met several times in the past.

I thought of calling the Chief of Police in Superior, however, I was trying to limit the people involved per the request of ICE officials.

"Sheriff, this is FBI Agent Mark Lawson. I have an emergency. How quickly can you get an unmarked car to the Superior Midwest Energy coal terminal?

"I have a person under surveillance with all our resources in use. I need a tail. One more thing, they can't use the police radio, it may be monitored."

"I'm just finishing a late lunch about six blocks away, and I'm in an unmarked car. What do you need?" he inquired.

"I'm on top the General Mills grain terminal. I have a person in a Coast Guard uniform that may have critical evidence on him. He has us split two ways already, and I am too far away to get to my car. Can you tail him if I give you a description from up here on my perch as to his route?"

"Stay on the line," he told me, "I just left someone a heck of a tip, covering my burger with a twenty on the table, as I left the diner. I'm not far away."

The man in the Coast Guard uniform slowly walked down the dock and got into a car. I got his photo and the license number of his grey Toyota Camry. I relayed the information to the chief, who told me he was four blocks away in a black Ford Escape.

From my bird's nest, I could see the black Escape as the Sheriff rounded a corner and caught up to the Camry near the exit of the coal terminal. He was following it from almost a block.

I watched the ship until the Calvin Wroth pulled away from the dock. I didn't want any more surprises.

Then, I scrambled down to the ground, got into my car, and followed the directions given by Sheriff Bernaski, as to which way our Coast Guard man was heading.

As I sped down the road, I called Agent Olson.

I filled him in on what I observed and how I had asked the Douglas County Sheriff, Rick Bernaski, to assist us without using his radio.

We had been split up too many ways by this operation and we needed the added support.

I told him I would keep him informed if anything changed with our suspects. My other agent was still on his tail.

Agent Olson told me he would do the same with his man.

Chapter 21

Games

It had been the perfect shell game. One of the oldest tricks in the books and we almost fell for it. The pea had been shuffled under the three shells. The question was in the hand; which shell held the treasure.

Stubby had indicated to me that I should follow the third person. Without communications, I was at a loss as to why he figured the third person held the evidence.

I was still wondering where he had been the hour he was out of sight.

Still, we had three suspects we needed to follow. Without any evidence, and without showing our presence, we needed to treat all three as our prime suspects.

Agent Olson was still watching the tow truck. It had been deserted at a towing company parking lot. Because of several people in the area, he could not approach it without someone seeing him.

If the evidence was still in the tow truck, he needed to watch to see who retrieved it. He had a pair of field glasses trained on the truck.

My FBI agent was still following the car that left with an individual that had resembled Paul Radcliff. With all that had happened in the past two hours, it might be him, or it might be someone else.

Until he stopped somewhere, we would not know. Until then, I told him to stick close.

Sheriff Bernaski was following the third suspect. The suspect drove to a warehouse on the St. Louis River, just south of town.

The odds were he was not an employee of the Coast Guard. If he was a Coast Guard employee, his job title probably wouldn't survive the day.

I caught up to Sheriff Bernaski just a few minutes after he had pulled over and parked about six hundred feet from the warehouse.

After pulling my car in behind him, I slipped into the passenger seat of the Sheriff's car to find out what he had seen.

"Well Agent Lawson, tell me, what do we have here? You didn't exactly give me a full briefing while I was leaving my half-pound cheeseburger with fries on the platter."

"I appreciate it Rick. I owe you one.

"Customs has been tracking a smuggler for some time. They had a tip that they were going to use the Calvin Wroth, on its trip to the Duluth harbor, to smuggle something into the U.S. I was told it was supposed to be some sort of painting, and we assumed it would be in a tube.

"You see, they played the old shell game on us.

"After staging a diversion, a man came off the ship with a tube. Our regional Customs agent followed him, while I kept an eye on the ship from my bird's nest on top the elevator.

"To my surprise, a second person came off the ship with an identical tube. I had one of my local FBI agents tail that one while I waited for the ship to sail.

"Just as it was about to leave, our man in the Coast Guard uniform comes off the boat with a third tube.

"I knew I couldn't get to my car in time, so I called you. If you didn't have anyone close, I was going to call the Chief of Police in Superior to see if he had a car available. I figured I could keep eye contact on the car for several blocks from up on top of the elevator, plus I had the license plate number."

"OK, at least you didn't offer me some road kill this time. What would you like to do?" he asked.

"I'm going to find a spot where I can watch the rear of the building as well. If you could watch the front until we get some backup, I would appreciate it."

"It will cost you two cheeseburgers and perhaps some onion rings," he told me.

"Deal. But, only if you can get me some info on this building. We need to know who we are dealing with."

Leaving my car where it was parked, not to create any more attention than necessary, I moved to a spot in the parking lot two buildings away that offered a view of the backside of the building we were watching, as well as a view of anyone turning into the front of the building.

I was hoping that either Agent Olson or my FBI agent would call me to say they concluded their observation.

This group was good. They knew how to string out any surveillance.

As I found a good observation point from the one parking lot where I could stay hidden, I received a call from the Sheriff.

"Mark, this is Rick. I have some info for you on the building. The city has it listed as a warehouse. Three employees. The last fire inspection was six months ago, so they have a building map if you need it."

That was good news. I was hoping we didn't have to tail thirty employees as they left work. We were still short manned based on the tactics they used earlier.

I asked Sheriff Bernaski if he could spare a couple more cars if we needed them. He told me that he would have them nearby.

Now, it was looking like a waiting game. Who would move first? I called Agent Olson and gave him the updated info on our surveillance. I told him it was his call as for what he wanted to do next.

Agent Olson had kept in touch with his agents in New Jersey. What had originally appeared as a simple tail had become a complex shell game, and the agents in New Jersey were worried that things were falling apart once again. With all the intel they had prior to the ship docking, they really didn't want to take a chance of losing the evidence. If nothing moved in the next couple of hours, someone would be stuck with the decision of which location and how they wanted to proceed. It was obvious that they really wanted to catch the entire operation at once. If they had to move in now, anyone downstream in the operation would be gone.

The first move came with the tow truck. Agent Olson spotted a man climb into the truck, turn on its emergency lights, and pull out on the road. He followed from a distance.

It was heading south – out of town on Highway 35.

Agent Olson put a call into me. "Agent Lawson, can you ask the Sheriff if he has a report of an accident south on Hwy 35? The truck has his lights on, and it is heading south."

I quickly called the Sheriff.

"Rick, Customs Agent Olson said the tow truck has its lights on and is heading south on Hwy 35. Any accidents out that way that may need a truck?"

"That's a 10-4. I just heard about a car in the ditch about six miles south of town. We have a car there."

"Great! When the tow gets there, can the deputy look for a cardboard tube in the cab, without being noticed?

"Also, have them watch for any handoff. Agent Olson will be following the truck with his pickup, so he'll keep an eye on the driver as well, once he gets there.

"You will have to call your deputy on his phone. They may be monitoring the air waves."

"Sounds like a plan. Anything moving in your view?"

Still quiet I told him, as I hung up and relayed a text message with the information to Agent Olson.

The Sheriff's deputy had located his cruiser on the shoulder of the highway, with the lights on, to warn on-coming traffic.

The car was off the road, in a muddy ditch, and would not be going anywhere until the tow came and pulled it out. Apparently, the driver had told the deputy that he swerved to miss a car that was over the centerline.

Other than being upset, he was fine.

As the tow truck arrived, he pulled his rig onto the shoulder ahead of the car in the ditch, and exited the truck to talk to the officer and owner of the car. Traffic was starting to rubberneck, which was slowing down the cars and causing a small backup on the highway in each direction.

This was working out fine for Agent Olson. As he got closer, he pulled over to the opposite side of the highway and made it look as though he was observing the operation.

While the tow operator was running his cable down to the car in the mud, the deputy asked the operator if he had an extra flair, he could put on the road to help traffic.

"Yeah, look behind my seat in the cab," he replied.

It was exactly what the deputy was hoping for. Quickly, he opened the door and looked for the flair as well as a cardboard tube. They were both there.

As he checked the tube by removing the endcap, he saw that it was full of blank paper.

The Sheriff's deputy walked down the road about one hundred feet and planted the lit flair in the middle of the road, so that when the car was pulled from the ditch, it would help with the traffic flow. On the way back, he passed the pickup truck he figured was Agent Olson's.

His window was down and Agent Olson quietly asked, "Anything in the cab?"

"Yes, however, the tube is full of blank paper. You want me to retrieve it for you?

"No. Thanks! That's what we needed to know. I'll put a good word into the Sheriff for you."

As he told him that, Agent Olson pulled back onto the highway.

After making a U-turn, and waiting for an opening in the traffic flow, he headed back towards the other operations still in progress.

Chapter 22

Stake Outs

Customs Agent Olson called me as soon as he cleared the traffic.

"Mark, Olson here. The tow truck turned out to be a ruse. The deputy slipped into the cab and the tube was filled with blank paper. I'm heading back.

"Think I should head for your location, or your other agent's location?"

I informed him, "I just talked to him a few minutes ago. You know that cut-off to Duluth, where the double decker bridge is? He's about a mile east of the bridge at a bar.

"The suspect got out of his car and went inside without the tube. On top of that, my agent felt he must have had a mask on. He probably removed it while he was on the road.

"He's in the bar watching him right now. The guy is pretty loose and not acting like he is waiting for anyone."

"I got a text from Stubby. Radcliff's still onboard. He must have passed the tubes on to a dock worker," Agent Olson told me.

"Well if he left the tube inside the car in that neighborhood, I don't think he is our guy. Can your agent stay with him for a while?"

"No problem. I told my agent you were picking up his beer tab. I think our man is the one at my location."

"Why don't you head this way. You can relieve the Sheriff. I'm sure he has other work to do. If he stays longer, I'll owe him two steak dinners."

"Okay. See you in fifteen minutes," Olson told me.

I called Sheriff Bernaski and told him the progress we were making as well as how well his deputy pulled off the search.

"Rick, Agent Olson will be here in fifteen minutes. When he gets here, you don't have to stay. I want to thank you for your help. I'll fill you in on the case when we get it closed over a good dinner.

"Oh, if you don't mind, can you leave those cars close just in case they play another game?"

"Depends. You picking the restaurant or me?"

"Thanks, your choice."

It took Agent Olson ten minutes to arrive at the scene. Obviously, he had a lead foot. As he pulled up, the Sheriff left.

It was good to have a different car watching the front side of the building. His pickup blended in looking like just another northern Wisconsin farmer.

My car was still on the street. However, with no one in it, it would not look threatening to anyone. The only problem, I was getting tired of standing outside, near the building. Soon, it would be the end of the day and people would be getting off work. I would have to move before that.

I was just about to move into the brush behind the businesses when I noticed a car pull into the lot in front of the warehouse we were watching.

I called Agent Olson.

"Got him in sight," he responded. "One man. Just got out of his car, looked around and headed in the building. Might be our man."

He only stayed inside for ten minutes or less. When he came out, he looked down the street, put something in the trunk of a silver Hyundai and hopped into his car. From my location, it looked like a cardboard tube.

Decision time. Now, it was up to Olson if we picked up the individuals inside the building or if he just wanted to tail the car.

"Your call," I told him. "What do you want to do?"

"You got a good photo of the courier from the ship, and his license number didn't you?" he asked.

"Yes, but there is no guaranty it was a good plate or that he works there."

"Well, we can raid that place later. Right now, I'm worried that our suspect might call back there and find out we arrested someone.

"I'm guessing I might have a long drive from here. Probably straight to Chicago. I'll have some support coming on the route."

"Mark, I think I can handle it from here," he informed me, as he was pulling out to follow the car. "Thanks for all the help. I'll let you know what happens. Can you send me your photos?"

I told him I would wrap it up from here.

Just to make sure, I stopped at the warehouse and asked for directions to a location I looked up on the map on my cell phone. While I was talking to the people inside, I snapped a couple photos of them in the office with my cell phone. It would place them at the scene if we needed it later for evidence.

Then, I drove over to the bar where my agent was sitting, watching our other suspect.

I wasn't sure if our agent could legally drive home or not after sitting there at the bar that long.

Arriving at the bar, I looked in the car to see if I could spot the cardboard tube. It was lying on the back seat of the car. One more observation; the doors were not locked.

This was nothing more than a rabbit for us to chase. Olson had the right person.

I sat down with my agent. He had only ordered one beer and it was still half-full. Our suspect was still sitting at the end of the bar.

My agent told me that he would stay until our suspect left and follow him home. He had run his plates and knew the direction the suspect should be heading.

The suspect only lived a couple miles down the road. If no one approached his car before then, it was probably time to turn him loose.

I agreed with his assessment.

Before heading out of town, I stopped by Sheriff Bernaski's office and told him a little more about the case. I figured I owed him that along with a dinner.

I think he was surprised as well as pleased that I stopped in at his office. It seemed that every time we were involved with a case, I had to withhold information from him. This time, I gave him the full story, including the fact that the case was tied into the shooting out on the gravel road, some time ago.

I told him that he had to keep that part to himself.

Bernaski was glad to finally know what was going on in his territory. Now, he could put a little logic into the event, even though he still did not have a clue as to the shooter's identification.

Bernaski was too busy for dinner that night, so we left it open for the next time I was in town or when he got down to the cities.

It was a long ride back to Minneapolis. I kept wondering how the case would turn out. I hoped that Agent Olson and his Customs agents would find the next leads in the case.

The list of characters in this caper seemed to be getting longer and longer.

I didn't envy Stubby O'Shea on the Calvin Wroth. The stormy season was upon us and, personally, I wasn't one for big waves. I was sure he was hoping the case would come to a quick close.

Chapter 23

Cross Linking

The next morning, I had just settled into my chair in my office, when I got a phone call.

"I think we found a few links," my agent told me. She had been monitoring the cell phones between Canada, Two Harbors, Duluth and Superior. Somehow, she had found the dotted lines linking a couple calls that were involved in the smuggling case.

I told her I would stop down to her office as soon as I poured a cup of coffee.

Our electronics/communications expert's office was two floors below mine. I was wondering what she had found in the lists of phone calls made to and from those regions over the course of a couple of days.

I was always amazed when I walked by her office. She had four monitors. Two were in front of her, while on each side was another one, angled slightly to give the appearance there were four monitors for her screen. How she handled it, I did not know. I had enough problems handling the screen on my cell phone.

As I walked into her office, she greeted me with a broad smile and said, "Your hunch paid off."

After five minutes of listening to her tell me how she cross-linked the data from forty different cell towers attempting to find data that linked to either the old phone numbers we had gathered, or linking to the time of the event at the Duluth harbor; I stopped her.

"Wow, let's get to the chase. What did you find?" I asked.

"Well, nothing seemed to make sense, that is until I found one call that originated in Superior, right at the coal terminal, which was made to Toronto.

"As I looked at a time sequence from that call, I was able to put together six calls in the next ten minutes."

"Okay, but what do we have?" I asked.

"Three of the calls were made from registered cell phones. The other three were from burner phones. One of those I linked back to the evening before your shooting in northern Wisconsin. Interested?"

"All right, you got my attention. So, we have phone calls. How can we trace them to the callers?"

"Remember how your caller in Sault Ste. Marie used their regular phone plus a burner phone, giving us a name and location? The phone they called was the one used in Toronto.

"That was the phone number that person in Superior called from, the phone we identified near the coal terminal, and the same phone used on your other case."

"Wait a minute. You saying the shooter from the corn field, on that gravel road, was at the coal terminal in Superior?" I interjected.

"I can't tell that for sure. But, the phone was," she explained.

It was their second mistake. They should have discarded it after the last use. I thought about it for a minute.

"Can you tell me where they were?" I asked.

"Absolutely! It appears the cell was across from the entrance gate at the coal terminal. The other burner that called it was on the ship."

I quickly realized, they had protection in place in case we figured out their game. If I was right, they had a shooter ready to take out anyone following the car with the real evidence coming out of the terminal.

"What time were the calls?" I asked. Can you run a timeline between my cell phone calls from the grain terminal and theirs?"

She nodded. Three minutes later, she hand me a list. She had them side by side.

As I looked at the calls I made to Agent Olson, it gave me a reference for what was going on in front of us, and when they were monitoring our actions.

Three calls were made from the ship.

One - when the truck had engine problems.

One - when the man that looked like Radcliff came out of the ship.

In addition, one - at the time the Coast Guard person left the ship.

They were watching all of them. They probably knew we followed the first two people.

Had they missed the fact that we had a tail on the last one?

I thought about it for a minute. The Sheriff was in an unmarked car. Plus, he came from the other direction and was blocks behind the man as he exited the coal terminal. They never saw him.

If I had managed to run to my car to follow them, the man with the burner might have been waiting for me to follow. If I had, he might have made sure that no one was following and....

We got lucky. They had the insurance card.

Turning back to my expert, I asked her, "How's your ability to enlarge photos and resolution?"

"Can't do anything on forwarded cell calls," she informed me, "just photos."

"Can you pull a photo off my computer and blow it up?" I suggested.

"If you give me the link."

Less than a minute later, she had remotely logged into my computer. I gave her directions to my current file.

"Go to my photos from yesterday. Now, scan for the time I called the Sheriff and copy the photos from there until fifteen minutes later."

It didn't take her long. That was the time interval I was scoping the suspect, and letting the Sheriff know exactly where he was.

"There – can you zoom in on the opposite side of the gate – just to the right, the direction where the car is going to turn."

As she did, I could see someone standing next to a truck as the car exited the terminal. It was a long photo, but we could make it out with the aid of her enhancing software.

On one photo, there was a glimmer next to his hand.

"Damn. He did have a gun," I told her.

"Crop it in as far as you can without losing resolution and save it, plus make me a print. Then, look for any of the photos I shot that gets a clear image of his face. Perhaps a license number on that truck as well."

When we were done, we hit the jackpot. It was weak evidence, but my guess was that we had our shooter from the other case.

If the Sheriff could find him with the burner phone, we could probably pin him for the murder even if they discarded the original gun. If he still was using the gun, they had him for sure.

I congratulated my agent. There was a chance that she had found something that might crack the case. It was a big feather in her cap.

As soon as I got back up to my desk, I contacted Sheriff Bernaski. "Sheriff, this is Agent Lawson, I've got some interesting news for you."

I proceeded to let him know what we discovered, including the fact that he was almost a target of the shooter from our previous case.

"I'm not sure if I should thank you or demand a higher payment," Sheriff Bernaski chided me. "I didn't know your interesting news was that you were using me as a target."

He thanked me for the new information and told me that he would start looking for the person as quickly as possible.

I reminded him that we needed to bring down the whole case at the same time.

"We'll try," he told me.

Chapter 24

Interference

Customs Agent Olson – Somewhere between Superior, Wisconsin and Chicago

Customs Agent Olson was leading the active tail of his suspect, whose car was on a highway heading towards Chicago. With the aid of a couple other Customs agents, they took turns keeping active surveillance on the suspect. This was one person they did not want to lose on the road.

Somewhere just before Madison, Wisconsin Agent Olson received a phone call from his boss.

"We just got a message from agents in China," Agent Kyle Easton of the New Jersey ICE office informed him. "They said they picked up information from their sources of another package from North Korea that may be headed to North America. This group is very active."

"They work quickly, Agent Olson told them. "Are you going to let that package get through before you take the "organization" down?"

"We are assessing the situation as we speak. Homeland Security is heavily involved as well. I just wanted you to know that the "organization" probably has no clue we are on to them if they are trying to bring across another package so quickly."

"Well, that's a good sign. Anything else?"

"Yes, we'd like to have you back off slightly. If we lose your man, we may have a second shot at them. We don't want to spook them into hiding right now."

"I understand," Agent Olson told him. "I'll keep you informed. Let me know if anything changes."

It was an unusual request. Normally, it would be rare to ask an agent to back off a known suspect with the thought that they might have a chance at another suspect in a few days or weeks.

Olson wasn't sure how to read the mixed messages coming from New Jersey. Something was going on and he felt as though he was definitely not in the direct loop.

This was not the way to run surveillance on a group suspected of murder.

They followed their suspect to a motel about thirty miles west of Chicago. Now, depending on the suspect's schedule, it was assumed that sometime in the next day or two the drawing would be delivered to the highest bidder.

The only question left standing – would the transfer be to another "organization" member, or to their buyer?

Theoretically, as far as Agent Olson was concerned, this case might be drawn to a conclusion by the end of the week.

Agent Mark Lawson

I got a message on my cell phone marked urgent. It was from Sheriff Rick Bernaski. I called him back as soon as I could.

"Rick, this is Agent Mark Lawson, you calling to collect on your free dinner already?"

"Your lucky day," he told me. "I've got a lead on that gunman you had me pose for, up at the terminal. Interested?"

"All ears, Rick. What did you find out?"

Sheriff Bernaski told me how he had several of his deputies stop in the local watering holes and ask the bartenders if they recognized the fuzzy photo I had taken from the top of the grain terminal.

One of the deputies got lucky and the bartender thought it was a guy that came in occasionally, usually in the evenings.

He told me, "I just wanted to know if you wanted to be in on the bust, or just pay me for another meal?"

I suggested to him, "You know, I think all the cheese is going to your head up there. Soon you will be wanting my job."

"Well, it sounds like it comes with a better expense account than we have up here. What's your preference?"

I told him I would like to be there when they pull him in. The only problem was they didn't know his name or when he would go back to the bar.

The license plate number we got from the photos did not have all the numbers. If we pulled him in, and the license had most of his numbers on it, we could use it for evidence.

However, we could not use it to go the other direction on finding him.

"Rick, I guess I'll stay loose down here until you have another sighting. I'm just glad to hear that he might be a local. Can you send me a text when you spot him?"

"Sounds good. I'm about to pull a John Doe search warrant on him, for when we spot him. I think the judge will grant us one based on the photo's you gave me. A man standing beside the road with a gun in his hand and a partial license plate will give him justification if we can match his face.

"Personally, I'm hoping we can find this shooter's gun. I'd like to put him away."

"Great, just be careful. The Fed's will be unhappy if we tip him off and he warns the "organization" before they are ready to drop their net. We might have to tiptoe here for a couple days until they are ready."

I asked Rick, "You don't suppose you can put him in a cell for a couple days because he ran out of the bar without paying his tab when you approached him?"

"You've been reading too many of those cheap novels again. Wish it worked that way. Okay, surveillance only as far as we feel it is safe without losing him. Perhaps we'll get lucky and he'll pull up in the same truck. Then, we can get his name and check his background, while we are watching him. I'll send you a text when we spot him."

"Thanks. You made my day," I told him.

I was wondering if our man in Wisconsin would turn up again or not. The fact that he was involved in two events in northern Wisconsin gave me the slim hope that he was possibly semi local.

Just to show that I was playing by the rules, I sent a note to New Jersey telling them that we were following up on a lead to see if we could identify the shooter of their first Customs agent in northern Wisconsin.

I didn't mention anything in my note that the lead came from the photos I had taken from the top of the grain terminal. I figured that might upset them, once again, that I was interfering in their case.

Later in the day, I got an acknowledgement. They had received my note.

The very next day, when I was thinking it was strange that I hadn't heard from Agent Olson since he headed off for Chicago tailing his suspect, I got a message from Sheriff Bernaski.

"Mark, we got a tip from a bartender that the shooter just showed up at the bar. I sent one of my off duty deputies over to mark him. I'll have another deputy check the parked cars nearby.

"Your call. Want us to pick him up or follow him?"

I sent a quick reply:

"Follow from a distance. Remember, he is an expert shot.

"Let me know if you get a confirmation on him. I'll head up then."

About an hour later, I got a response. It was definitely the man in the photo.

I grabbed my go-bag and headed for Superior. I figured that Sheriff Bernaski would have the lowdown on him by the time I arrived in town.

On the way up to Superior, Wisconsin, I kept thinking about what it would take to tie him to the cases.

Unless we found his gun, it would be hard to make any charges stick. The evidence that he had talked to someone in

Canada and that he was standing outside the coal terminal gate would not be grounds for an arrest.

No, we needed his gun. Would he have it with him, or was it hidden? Since he had not thrown it away earlier, perhaps he had it in a place close to him.

I just needed to work out a strategy.

First things first. We needed to find out who this suspect is, and run a background on him. Let's find out who we are dealing with.

Chapter 25

Suspects

I was glad it was only a two and a half hour drive to Superior from Minneapolis. I made it in exactly two hours.

I might have shaved another five minutes off the trip, except crossing the super high Blotnik Bridge, which crossed over the Duluth/Superior harbor, I was afraid that a gust of wind might cause my car to go airborne at the speed I was traveling. I wasn't sure if Sheriff Bernaski would like to take time out to fish me out of the water near the grain terminals.

As I was approaching the harbor, Sheriff Bernaski called me to fill me in on the situation.

He told me that the suspect appeared to be getting ready to leave the bar. His deputy was shadowing him just as we discussed earlier.

Also, they found the suspect's car. Running the license plate, they came up with a driver's license with our suspect's photo on it. Now, provided the info was correct, we might have connected a name and address to our suspect.

I could tell by Sheriff Bernaski's voice that he had developed an invested interest in this case.

"How sure are you of the info?" I asked the Sheriff.

"Well, let's put it this way. I could have been in his sights the other day. We're going to know everything about him by the time you pull in, including the day of the week he was born."

Rick was right. If he had been in a marked car that day, things could have taken a very different course.

Sheriff Bernaski had me meet him about two blocks away from the bar. He was sure the suspect was about to pay his tab, but he had no idea which direction he would go once he left the bar. The address he obtained from his license plate might be fake.

I joined him in his car.

"Quick trip. I take it you didn't stop for dinner on the way up?" he joked.

"I thought you said you were buying? Thanks for letting me know our suspect was here. I'm just anxious to finally see the guy.

"Now that we know who he might be, we need to figure out a way to get something on him. Any suggestions?" I asked.

"Well, I pulled some strings and got an open search warrant on him. That way we can execute it when you give us the go-ahead. What do you think we'll find? Rick asked me.

"As I look at it, we really need that hand gun. If it is the same gun, it's too bad we didn't know he had it on him the other day. We could have pulled him over and searched his car.

"I don't think he is sloppy enough to carry it on him. The shooting looked too professional. He may have another gun in his car.

"We need to be careful. Any sign of a concealed carry permit in his name?"

"Running a check on it as we sit here," the Sheriff answered.

I took the information he had gathered so far, and ran it by my office to see if they could pull any additional information on the suspect. We were looking for any clues we could use.

The suspect came out of the bar and got into his car.

The deputy called the Sheriff and fed him the information as to which way he was heading. So far, the deputy was about a block behind him in his car.

Fortunately, rush hour traffic was over and the streets of Superior Wisconsin were partially deserted. As a result, the deputy needed to keep a full block between them to keep from being noticed.

After a mile, he arranged for another car to take the lead following the suspect's car.

Sheriff Bernaski and I were about three blocks behind them just in case they felt they were spotted.

The good news was that it appeared as if he was heading towards the address listed on his license. The bad news was that it was ten miles east of town on Highway 2, heading towards Ashland. That was open road.

We had to back off almost a mile to keep from being spotted, and had to switch leads twice before he got to his house.

When he turned into the farmhouse, located in the woods, we continued on the highway for another mile, before turning around.

"Alright," Sheriff Bernaski said, "we have an ID, and now a confirmed address. What would you like to do next? You want to check out his house? If we don't find anything, you've kind of tipped your hat."

The Sheriff was right. Pulling the search warrant may have been premature. We needed another solution.

"Rick, how often did that bartender say he went to the bar?"

"Every couple days, usually around 4 to 5 pm. Sometimes two days in a row. Why?"

"This guy probably takes pride in his shooting. I'm not suggesting that you pick a fight with him, and see if he draws a gun. However, what if we have someone bait him into shooting a wolf, while he is taking a sip at the bar? I'll bet he would jump for the thought of shooting a wolf for someone for a price. What's your thoughts?"

"It would give us an excuse to investigate him if he agreed. You thinking he might bring his gun?"

"We'll need to lead him that way. I think he might if we tell him he can't use a rifle. Too many other animals in the area. If he uses another handgun, we can still check out his place using that warrant. He won't even know."

We left one of his deputies to keep watch on the farmhouse from a distance, while Rick and I went for dinner. Rick picked the place for their tender steaks.

By the time Rick was done relishing his German chocolate cake for dessert, we had a plan.

We would bait him at the bar with a female who could weave a story about how a wolf was raiding her henhouse, and was looking for someone that was a good enough shot to kill it.

I suggested to him that we might be able to use a deputy sheriff from Minnesota, so that the suspect wouldn't accidentally recognize her.

I had one in mind that I thought could handle the conversation.

When we left the restaurant, it was all set. Besides having a lighter wallet, I had made a call to Deputy North. She agreed to go undercover and be our bait for the next couple of days.

She sent a message to her boss with the pertinent information and that the FBI had asked for assistance. Her boss gave her a quick okay.

Sheriff Bernaski had a relative with a farm just outside of town. After a phone call, it was all set. We could use the farm for the sting.

If we played our cards right, the suspect wouldn't even know why he was picked up.

Now, after a little prep work, all we needed to do was hope that our suspect showed up at the bar.

Chapter 26

The Collar

Chicago – Customs Agent Olson

Customs Agent Olson had trailed his smuggling suspect from Superior, Wisconsin all the way to the outskirts of Chicago, Illinois. As he was hoping to wrap up his surveillance in a day or two, he had received word from Agent Kyle Easton, in New Jersey, that there might be further complications, and to back off slightly. They wanted to reassess the case before cracking it open with an arrest.

This had been a tough case to work on ever since the start. For Agent Olson, it seemed that everyone in law enforcement knew more about the case than he did. He was frustrated.

According to the intelligence Customs had received, their suspect was expected to deliver a rare drawing to a client the following day. Now, Olson was waiting word whether he should arrest the suspect and the recipient of the smuggled goods, or simply monitor the sale.

On top of that, he had received word from FBI Special Agent Mark Lawson that he had a suspect in the previous murder of a Customs agent. Agent Olson was eager to close his case.

That night, he had a conference call with the agents in New Jersey as well as Agent Farley in Homeland Security.

Agent Olson asked, "Can you let me know what's going on? I think we can wrap this up tomorrow and now it looks like someone is dragging their feet. What's up?"

"Sorry Olson, this is Agent Farley. Something came up yesterday here in Washington and depending on the decisions made; it may delay your case.

"I was discussing it with the CIA. We think there might be a chance we could use these people in a bigger case if we were able to talk to them and offer them something in return, instead of years in prison.

"I'm not talking about all of them, just a small select few. However, if we show our hand in the case you are working too early, they might go underground and our chances are lost."

"So, where does that leave me? What should I do tomorrow when the package gets delivered? We either catch them in the process or we might lose it," Olson responded.

"We need to delay things a day. I'll leave that to you, but somehow, you need to delay the handoff for one day while we work out our details"

Olson groaned. How? Walk right up to them and offer them a poker game instead of handing the package to someone for several thousand dollars?

"Can you handle that?" Agent Easton asked.

"I'll delay it. As for how long, that I can't predict. Get your discussions done quickly, so we can stop playing games with these people."

Agent Olson talked it over with the rest of his surveillance team. The question was; how do you stop someone without tipping your hand to them?

The next morning, about 10:00, their suspect appeared to be getting ready to check out of the motel. He was putting his luggage in the trunk of his car.

Olson and his team had an idea the evening before. Now, they hoped it would work without looking as though it was something planned.

The suspect drove over to the office of the motel to check out. He didn't appear to be in any great hurry. That probably meant that he was meeting his client either during the lunch hour or just after lunch.

He got back into his car after checking out of his room and drove to the exit. As he was looking to see if any cars were coming, he didn't even see it coming. A garbage truck made the left turn right in front of him, heading into the motel. Unfortunately, there wasn't room for two vehicles in the exit, especially when one was as large as a garbage truck.

The front of the truck just cleared the car. However, with a loud crunch, the rear end of the turning truck, including its rear wheels, struck the front left fender of the suspect's Hyundai Sonata car, as the truck tried to turn into the motel. The car was definitely pinned under the truck. The truck had come to an immediate stop; however, the damage was done.

Looking at the car, the front fender, headlight, grill, and probably the steering suspension was damaged. It was hard to tell what else might be damaged.

The truck driver jumped out of his truck, checked on the health of the driver of the car, and immediately tried to apologize for the accident. Other people, stopped by the truck blocking the road, started to gather, checking out the accident. Someone called 911 to report the accident.

Within a couple minutes, you could hear sirens as the police were reporting to the scene. It wouldn't take very long for them to arrive.

For the driver of the car, there was a definite problem. The accident had damaged the left front of his car. The car was pinned against the underside of the truck. With bucket seats and a consul, the driver couldn't just slide out the other side of his car. A small person might have been able to slither out of the situation. However, for a six foot three, two hundred and forty pound individual, slithering was only done in emergencies.

Realization came quickly. He was stuck in the driver's seat and would probably be there for some time, at least until someone moved his car, or the garbage truck.

Before the police arrived, he quickly phoned his prospective client, and tried to explain to him that a garbage truck had run into his car. As he explained the situation, it was decided that they would delay their meeting until the next day, when our suspect would have a rental car. Fortunately, the drawing was not damaged.

It was a good decision. No one knew how long the accident scene, and paperwork with the police, would take. The thought of taking a cab to the office building, with the drawing in hand, was not even considered.

After the police determined that no one was injured, even though the driver was still stuck inside his crumpled car, a wrecker was called to separate the vehicles. Someone had the idea of simply backing the garbage truck to free the car. However, it might have caused even more damage. They were wedged tight.

Due to the accident, traffic on the street in front of the motel was tied up for almost two hours.

Once the vehicles were separated, the suspect took the opportunity to stretch out his legs and went back into the motel to extend his stay for one more day. Before all the paperwork was completed with the police, he took a few minutes to empty out his vehicle, so that he could get a rental car, and allow the wrecker to haul his damaged vehicle away.

Fortunately, the damage was confined to the left front of the car and not to the back. The valuable drawing was not damaged and even more important, it was not discovered by the police.

The bad side of the event; the car really looked like a mess. It definitely was not one of his better days.

When everything cleared, he realized that he still needed to talk to the "organization" and explain why things had been delayed one day. A photo, sent from his burner cell phone, explained it the best. It had simply been beyond his control.

Once again, the cell call had been anticipated by Customs, and the numbers from the towers were monitored by law enforcement.

Agent Olson called Agent Kyle Easton in New Jersey and told him that the delay plan worked. They could trace the cell call to make sure the same individuals were involved. Hopefully, they would relay some marching orders from Homeland back to him shortly.

As he was waiting for new orders, his team observed the suspect signing for the rental car that had been delivered to the motel. It appeared that the suspect was all set to make his appointment the following day.

They needed a plan. Another delay planned for tomorrow, would be highly unlikely.

Chapter 27

Bait

Superior, Wisconsin – FBI Special Agent Mark Lawson

Everything was set. Sheriff Bernaski had talked to his relative and they agreed to let us use their farm for the sting. Deputy Alex North was given clearance from her Sheriff to take the necessary time away from her territory to be the bait for the sting. Even the bartender knew what was about to happen.

Now, we waited with anticipation for the suspect to show up at the bar and take the bait.

As an added bonus, I had talked to Art Swenson, from the Wisconsin DNR. He had agreed to be part of our team, and brought a tool for making wolf tracks to make the story more believable.

With him on board, and his expertise, it was starting to feel like the group we had for our pheasant-hunting trip. Only this time, we had a bigger target.

It was two days after the last time the suspect was in the bar when our surveillance team spotted him heading towards town.

By the time the suspect got to the bar, we were set up and ready.

Alex had put on some of her casual clothes that she would normally use when she went hiking in the woods. She was ready to play the part.

Alex watched from a table in the corner of the bar as the suspect came in and settled in a chair pulled up to the bar. He was dressed pretty casual looking as well.

Alex noticed that he was drinking beer, so she waited for him to drink at least three-fourths of the bottle before heading over to the bar.

She moved to about four-feet from where the suspect sat at the bar. There, in a sort of aggravated voice, slowly, she asked the bartender if he knew anyone that was a good shot. She told him that the past three nights a fox or small wolf had gotten into her henhouse, and gotten away with a couple of her prize chickens each time before she was able to get there to chase it away.

"That must be one brave animal to come back each night," she told the bartender. "The chickens make so much noise; you know something is out there. By the time I run the one hundred feet to the henhouse, all I see is a blur heading towards the woods and feathers all over the henhouse.

"I've got to do something. The hens aren't laying like normal. Another week and I'll be plum out of the egg business.

"I need to find someone that's a good shot that can hit a moving critter near dusk.

"There are other animals in the field, so I don't need a Rambo that takes twenty shots to hit the critter.

"You know anyone? Everyone I know is a scope shooter. That doesn't work very well when it is almost dark. My brother lives with me. The problem is; he can't even hit a pheasant."

We were listening in on a wire. So far, she sounded convincing to me. Even Sheriff Bernaski was impressed. Now, we hoped that the suspect would think of coming to the aid of the good-looking farmwoman.

"Well, off hand, I'm not sure I have any suggestions for you either," the bartender informed her. Most of the gents that come in here would probably shoot one of your bulls in your field after a few drinks, swearing it was a wolf in full stride.

"Have you tried the DNR? Sometimes they offer to help farmers with problem animals. Besides, if it is a wolf, you can't legally shoot them now anyway. However, the DNR could if they determine it is a problem animal. Give them a try."

"You think they would be willing to sit there for a couple hours, perhaps a couple days in a row to get it?" she asked him. "Heck, it would be worth it for me to pay someone $100 just to shoot it.

"Well, think about it. There must be someone around here that can hit what they aim at," she told the bartender, asking for another bottle of lite beer.

When she got her beer, she went back to the table in the corner. She sat there and slowly sipped on her beer.

So far, the suspect was not taking the bait. He just sat at the bar, drinking his beer and watching the television screen. They were playing replays of last week's Green Bay football game. He acted as though he never even heard the conversation.

The suspect was about half way through a second bottle of beer, when he stirred in his seat. Then, he slowly sauntered over to Alex's table.

"Excuse me miss, but I overheard your conversation with the bartender. You say you have animal problems?"

"Yes and that damn thing is going to take me out of the egg business. I'd love to take a turn with my shotgun at it, but I'd hit the animals in the field and probably miss the beast. It moves pretty fast when it hears me coming."

"What exactly is it?" he asked.

"I can't really tell for sure. Could be a big fox or a small wolf. Maybe a timber wolf. They are all over the area."

"You know, there are wolverines in the area too. They look a little smaller, but you definitely don't want to corner one, especially at night. I'd be a bit careful if I was you. Have you seen any tracks?"

"Tracks! Yes, they're all over the chicken coop and around my fence. I'm not a big game hunter, so I couldn't tell a German shepherd from a fox. You don't think it could be a dog do you? Can you tell by looking at the tracks? I could show you."

"Perhaps!" he answered.

"Do you know anyone that is a good shot? I need someone that can hit what they shoot at. I don't want to lose any of my farm animals in the field. Heck, at that time of the day, I'd probably shoot my cat while it was chasing a mouse. That would really solve my problems."

We were listening in, holding our breath. So far, Alex was doing a great job. Heck, I would even jump at the chance to volunteer to help her.

"I might be able to get rid of it for you," the suspect told Alex. "I would want to look at the tracks first, just to know what I'm up against."

"You really think you can do it? I could show you the tracks. Heck, that thing will probably be back there later this evening.

"When could you check it out?" she asked. "I'm tired of staying up to chase it away after it has robbed me of another chicken or two. It's the critter or me."

"Well, I'm not busy right now; if you want I could head over and check it out. Shouldn't take long to see what the thing is."

"Do you have a gun? I'm afraid a high powered rifle would hit something in my field or, well, my neighbor's house is probably in range of a good rifle," she inquired.

"My neighbor is only a few hundred feet from my place. I'd probably need to warn him that we were trying to catch my chicken thief. I told him about it, but he is too old to shoot anything in dim light. I had better warn him if there might be a gunshot. Otherwise, he might come running thinking I was trying to do my own shooting. He's kind of protective that way."

"I got a hand gun. How far from here do you live?" he asked.

"Only ten minutes down the road. Can you hit what you shoot at with a hand gun?"

"I think I could handle it," he answered.

The suspect was eating out of Alex's hands. He had Alex write down her address and directions on a napkin. Then, he told her that he would meet her at her place in an hour or so. After that, he headed to the restroom to drain off some the beer he had consumed.

When he came back out, Alex was gone. She had played her part perfectly.

She left in an old pickup parked in front of the bar that Sheriff Bernaski had supplied, just in case the suspect was watching her.

We watched as the suspect went back to his place. He was only there for a few minutes, and then, leaving his driveway, he headed towards the farm.

So far, we felt extremely lucky.

We had him admit that he had a handgun, he was a good shot, and he knew there were wolverines in the area. Now, we hoped that he had gone back to his place to get his favorite gun – the one he used to kill the Customs Agent on the gravel road.

Chapter 28

The Henhouse

We had to scramble once we knew there was a possibility that the suspect might be headed to the farm.

The owner of the farm, as well as their neighbor, was asked to leave for the evening. We didn't want any accidental contact with our suspect. Especially, since we knew the suspect might be armed.

It was bad enough that we had put Deputy Alex North in danger without a bulletproof vest on. I was hoping she could take care of herself. Besides, we would be extremely close, and she still had the wire on. The thought of a brother possibly in the house as well as the comment to the suspect that the neighbor was an old protective man that owned a gun might keep him in line as well.

Art Swenson, Sheriff Rick Bernaski and I set up in the attic of the farmhouse. If the suspect spotted any movement in the window, he would think it was the brother.

For additional support, I had a sharpshooter out in the woods, with night gear and scope. He was wrapped in a thermal blanket and would not turn his gear on until we gave him the word that the suspect was at the farm, and away from his vehicle. We didn't want him to scan the woods with a night scope and spot our man.

Everything was in place. That is, except for our suspect. According to our surveillance team's messages, he left his place and was headed towards us. It was not that far. He should have been here. Where was he?

About thirty minutes later, as his truck pulled into the driveway, we all took a sigh of relief. He took the bait.

As he pulled up near the house, Alex walked out to meet him. We could pick up the conversation from her wire.

"Sorry I was a little late. I decided to pick up some fast food on the way since I didn't have any supper. Steadies the old nerves.

"So, show me the tracks. Let's see what kind of animal we are looking for," he told her.

They walked over to the henhouse. It was getting dark and Alex had a flashlight to show him the tracks.

As they got to the fence around the henhouse, the suspect took the flashlight and pointed to a few tracks near a weak spot in the fence.

"See there! That's wolf tracks. In fact, those are timber wolf tracks, not brush wolf tracks. The DNR keeps calling them grey wolfs. I think they are trying to give them a better image.

"I hear the government is trying to make it legal to shoot them again on a limited season. Wish they would hurry up. They kill deer all winter to survive. A pack of them can kill ten to fifteen deer in a winter. That's why the deer population is dropping in the county."

"You mean we can't shoot it?" Alex asked.

"No, I just said we weren't supposed to. The way I see it, that wolf is creating problems with the farm animals. That makes it legal to shoot.

"Perhaps you might have lost a guard dog or cat that was used for killing mice in the barn?" he asked as if it really wasn't a question.

"Oh! I see. Yes, there have been a few animals missing lately. When do you think you could shoot it?" Alex asked.

"You did say that you would be willing to pay to have it shot didn't you?" he reminded her.

"Yes, I suppose I did. Yes, I told the bartender I would pay one-hundred dollars for anyone that could shoot it.

"When do you think you could get rid of it for me?"

"This looks like a good night. Let's move away from here so we don't leave any more scent in the area than we have already done. I'll get my jacket and gun out of the truck. Then I'll find a good hiding spot from the wolf. I'll let you stay in the house.

"If you'd like, maybe you could make some coffee so I could warm up after the animal is put down."

"That sounds like a good plan. I hope you have some luck," Alex told him, and headed back into the farmhouse.

As we watched from behind a set of curtains in the darkened room, the suspect took a heavy tan colored canvas-style jacket out of the truck along with his gun. Then, he found a corner, by the one shed, that gave him a good view of the henhouse. It would be about a sixty foot shot it he saw the animal.

He blended in perfectly with the dry weeds in the area. The yard light gave us just enough light to allow us to keep him under surveillance without using our infrared scopes.

Art Swenson turned to me. "Too bad we don't have one of those mechanical wolves. We could nail him for actually shooting at a wolf."

"This is almost as good. We have him on tape saying he is going to shoot a timber wolf for money.

"I'm not about to approach him with his gun drawn. I've seen his accuracy before. Let's wait him out. When he gets cold and tired of looking at the field, he'll come in for coffee. That's when we will take him down. Remember, you will have to be the arresting officer. This will be a DNR sting."

"With pleasure," Art answered.

All of us had to give him credit, our suspect stayed out in the cold until almost 10:30. Only then, we saw him put his gun in the truck and head in for coffee.

As he was let in the back door of the farmhouse to get some warm coffee by Deputy Alex North, Art Swenson surprised the suspect by coming in the side door to the kitchen.

"I'm DNR Officer Art Swenson," he told him. "I'm arresting you for attempting to illegally shoot a grey wolf. You have the right to remain silent. Anything you say may be used in a court of law."

"You can't prove anything. I was just watching for an animal that was raiding her henhouse," he responded. "Just ask the lady."

"Well, I hate to ruin your day, but Officer North is wired, so, we have your words on tape. I'll let your lawyer decide how innocent you are. For now, I am confiscating your gun and taking you in to the Sheriff's office to fill out the paper work. I suggest that you cooperate. The fine is far less than resisting arrest."

He was caught flat-footed and he knew it. Now, all he could do was act like the duped good guy that was trying to help a lady in distress. He needed to do whatever the arresting officer insisted.

Sheriff Bernaski had his deputy in the woods drive over to pick up the suspect. As he drove in, the Sheriff snuck out of the attic, and went out the front door, where he met the deputy at his car. He wanted to make it look as though he was arriving with his deputy.

They put the suspect in their car and took him to their office. DNR Officer Swenson followed.

Meanwhile, I had stayed hidden in the farmhouse. I didn't want to tip our suspect off that the FBI was involved.

After giving the owner and their neighbor the okay to come back home, and thanking them for their cooperation, I gave Alex a ride back to the hotel where she had been staying.

"You did great today," I told her. "You could have fooled me. Heck, I had all I could do to keep the Sheriff from coming to your aid and shooting the animal.

"Now, let's hope we get a match on that gun. If we do, he won't see the light of freedom for a long time. Shooting a federal agent will put him away for good."

"Thanks for letting me be part of this," Alex told me. "It is nice to see the conclusion of a case we opened."

"Well, if you ever get tired of driving those backroads of northern Minnesota and want to try a higher level job, you might want to send an application to our office. I think you would make a great FBI agent. We could use someone like you in our office."

"I just might keep that in mind," she answered, as we arrived at her hotel.

I thanked her for all the help and told her I would let her know if we had a perfect match on the gun or not.

Between Art Swenson and Sheriff Bernaski, they found some excuse to keep our suspect overnight.

When the gun turned out to have its serial numbers filed off, they kept him until the ballistics report came back.

It didn't take long, especially since they knew what they were looking for. The .38 caliber pistol was indeed a match to the ballistics from the killing on the gravel road, as well as the other unsolved killing on file. The grooves cut in the bullet by the machining of the barrel of the gun, were a perfect match.

Sheriff Rick Bernaski gave me a call. I could tell by the tone of his voice, he had a smile on his face.

"Mark, Sheriff Bernaski. Wanted to let you know right away. We got a match on the ballistics report. He's not going anywhere."

"Great. That's good news. Let me get a hold of Customs and Homeland and see how they want to proceed. For now, I think you will be able to add suspicion of murder to his log sheet."

After talking to Rick Bernaski for a while and thanking him for his help, I called Art Swenson and Alex North and thanked them for a job well done. Both were happy to have taken part in the conclusion of the case. It made up for our interrupted pheasant hunt.

Now, it was time to talk to Agent Farley at Homeland Security and the team in New Jersey to see if they wanted to connect our suspect with the rest of the smugglers.

So far, I had done exactly what I had promised. Our office had investigated the murder, identified the shooter, and kept it out of their bigger investigation.

As for the investigation into the death at the Two Harbors ore terminal, there was not enough evidence to prove murder even though everything pointed to an accidental death as part of a diversion in a smuggling case.

For now, we would have to leave that case as unsolved.

Chapter 29

Decisions

New Jersey Offices of Customs and Homeland Security

Conference calls between the Customs agents in New Jersey and Agent Farley in Homeland Security had been going on for two days, as the plans for picking up the "organization" all at one time seemed to change as often as the weather.

They knew that Customs Agent Olson was getting frustrated. He had followed their lead suspect to Chicago and as everything looked as though it was ready to come down, he had to find an excuse to delay the final connection of the art smuggling with a client.

On top of that, FBI Special Agent Lawson had worked the phone connections, capturing the killer of one or their Customs Agents by the "organization," by using the excuse of an attempted wolf kill.

Now, even the Canadian Customs officers were wondering what the holdup was on the program.

With both of these operations sitting on simmer, it was time to either bring down the curtain on the entire organization, or find another direction. Unfortunately, it was the later that Homeland was suggesting, and it was not sitting very well with Customs.

Apparently, there were high-level discussions going on the entire day before. They involved U.S., Canadian and Chinese officials. At stake was a possible source of secure information from North Korea.

It was well known that all three countries wanted to put an end to the organized smuggling gang that had been working through their countries. However, something more important had come up, and it required the agreement of all the countries to pull it off.

Just this morning, the heads of state of the three countries gave their final approval. Now, it was time to put the new plan in action.

Agent Farley explained to the Customs agents in New Jersey that a new plan had been worked out in Washington. They were still going to bring down the "organization." However, the CIA was becoming involved with the Chinese authorities in Hong Kong.

They wanted to work out a deal with the operator at the Chen-Lee Tea Company. For now, they wanted to keep that link alive while we shut down the rest of the "organization."

The owner of the Chen-Lee Tea Company had been picked up overnight (daytime in Hong Kong) as he headed to work. It was done in such a manner that no one else knew what happened.

When the Chinese authorities opened their books to the owner of the Chen-Lee Tea Company, showing him what they had on him, they gave him an option – life in prison or cooperation with the authorities in exchange for a lesser sentence.

It didn't take an expert to decide which door to pick.

The length of the sentence would be determined by the amount of cooperation he gave them. There were no lawyers present and very little options given.

By noon, an agreement was reached. He would surrender his passport, agree to be monitored at all times, and agree to run a controlled smuggling operation, directed by the Chinese government. However, it was agreed that no communications would be allowed to the "organization" members outside of China, and only a selected few within China would be involved. Any word of the cooperative operation leaking, and he would find himself in one of the worst prisons in all of China.

For all intensive purposes, the Chinese government had finally shut down the "organization" as it was presently running.

Now, it was up to Agent Farley to explain why they decided to let the Chinese smugglers off the hook and how he wanted the rest of the "organization" taken down.

It was decided that when Agent Olson confirmed that the transfer of the artwork to a client in Chicago was completed, in a coordinated operation; all the identified members of the "organization," in Canada and the United States would be picked up at the same time.

It would involve over fifty officers in several cities to successfully make the plan work. By taking down the "organization" at the same time, international charges could be applied as well as local charges. Smuggling, illegal money transfer, murder, and a few other charges would be applied to the whole group.

Several years of surveillance would finally pay off.

Customs Agent Kyle Easton, in New Jersey, asked him, "What's going on in Hong Kong that created all the new decision making?"

"Well, I hate to say this, but it's classified. Let's just say that we're hoping the drawings you followed from North Korea might provide us with the opportunity to get something more vital from there."

When you work for the government, the one thing you can't control is the information you really want to hear. The Customs agents knew they had just been dropped a hint, but until something hit the fan, it would probably be the last they would hear about it. It had become a part of the job.

There was definitely a pecking order and national security took precedent.

After their discussions, the go ahead was given to Agent Olson and his agents to round up his suspects in Chicago, including the purchaser of the smuggled artwork, once the purchase was completed.

Stubby O'Shea was notified, when he received the message, he could talk to the captain, and arrest Paul Radcliff on the Calvin Wroth.

The ship would be met by Customs when it docked at its next port. At that point, Radcliff would be taken off the ship.

FBI Special Agent Lawson was informed that when everything went down, he could connect his suspect with the smuggling group as well. After killing a Federal Agent, it probably would not add to his sentence, but perhaps they could get additional information out of him on the "organization."

Chicago – Customs Agent Olson

Customs Agent Olson was happy to hear that the bust would proceed as planned. He really didn't like having to stall things. Any attempt for a second delay, had the earmarks of disaster.

Once again, about 10:00 a.m., his team observed the suspect pack up his rental car and check out of the motel.

The deal was on. This time, there were no garbage trucks on the street as the suspect exited the driveway.

They followed him to a restaurant near O'Hare Airport. There, the suspect went in and took a booth. One agent went inside while others waited in cars outside.

Thirty minutes later, a man in a suit came in to the restaurant and sat down at the suspect's table. He was carrying a briefcase.

They had a cup of coffee together, and then after paying the bill, they left the restaurant.

The two of them walked directly to the suspect's rental car.

The suspect opened the trunk and handed the tube to the man in the suit. At the same time, the briefcase traded hands and was placed inside the trunk.

We watched as the suspect opened the briefcase and inspected its contents. It was full of cash.

Before he had a chance to close the trunk, the Customs agents quickly closed in.

It only took just a few minutes. There was no commotion or resistance. Both the currier and the buyer were caught flat-footed with the goods in hand.

Agent Olson checked the tube.

When he carefully opened the tube and unwrapped its contents, he admired the Tang Dynasty drawing. It definitely did not look like something drawn in the 700's AD. He wondered which museum would end up with the expensive drawing. The goal of the team was to return any artifacts to the rightful country or owners.

It was as close as the suspect's client would come to his purchase.

Agent Olson further inspected the buyer's briefcase. Inside, he found that the briefcase was full of hundred-dollar bills.

Obviously, it would make it easier for the "organization" to disburse the cash, than trying to cash a check made out to the "organization."

As a result of the takedown, both men were arrested and taken into custody. Their lawyers would be busy once they were booked at the courthouse.

Agent Olson notified the other agents that the takedown had been completed in Chicago, which started the ball rolling in the other cities.

The smuggling organization didn't even have time for a warning call. All the major "organization" locations were hit within the same hour. Only one or two individuals were missed in the sting. Those individuals were picked up within a few hours.

Onboard the Calvin Wroth, U.S. Customs Agent Stubby O'Shea, disclosed to Captain Taccetta that he was a Customs Agent and was working on a smuggling case ever since he came onboard the Calvin Wroth.

After disclosing to Captain Taccetta the evidence they had gathered on Engineer Radcliff, the Captain had Radcliff arrested for international smuggling.

Radcliff was put in handcuffs and locked in a holding area of the ship until they reached port.

Later that day, minor individuals were also rounded up in places such as Superior Wisconsin, Sault Ste. Marie, and several other cities. Most of these suspects would be charged with misdemeanors for their assistance of the smugglers.

The takedown of the "organization" went just as planned. The only thing that changed from the original plan was the lack of the big announcement.

Newspapers in several cities ran short articles in the back pages of their papers, announcing that several people had been arrested for smuggling. However, they never did attempt to tie the reports to the other cities where similar operations had taken place at the same time.

They intentionally kept it low key for the international news.

By the end of the week, probably the happiest one of the group was Stubby O'Shea. With the end of the case, he could finally get off the Calvin Wroth, before he had to endure another winter blast.

It had definitely been an experience; however, it was time to leave.

When Captain Taccetta reported to his head office that one of his crew had been arrested for smuggling and was removed from the ship at the port, he also notified them that they would need a second replacement. It was for U.S. Customs Agent Stubby O'Shea.

With the case closed, Stubby packed his sea bag. He said good-bye to the friends he had made on the ship, including Swede, Blackie, and the crew in the mess, before leaving the ship.

Now, Stubby was looking forward to another assignment – preferably back on one of the docks.

Chapter 30

The Proposal

Washington DC – Offices of the CIA and Homeland Security

Since the end of World War II, North Korea had been a problem for the U.S., South Korea, and Japan. It was the result of the splitting of Korea into North and South Korea. The division caused many problems.

After World War II, North Korea had turned into a military state and was using threats to bargain for food. It had close connections with China and Russia for purchasing food and materials needed.

On top of that, it had been used by Russia as its active arm for disrupting the west. Russia had supplied North Korea with arms and the training for how to disrupt the western economies way of life. With the loss of Cuba as its destabilizing arm for free economies, North Korea became one of Russia's sponsored countries.

When word reached CIA headquarters that Tang Dynasty drawings had been smuggled out of one the secret rooms of the Grand People's Study House in North Korea, the operations room in the Pentagon started to churn.

The CIA had been working for more than twenty years trying to secure information on the locations of secret workings within the confines of North Korea.

Most of the clandestine workings of North Korea were done in underground locations. Some in sub-basements, as in the Grand People's Study House.

Others were hid in tunnels dug deep between buildings to hide their operations form spy satellites. The goal was to make the operations more secure from foreign military interference.

Most of world was aware that North Korea had a nuclear program. With North Korea working with Iran and Russia, the program had the direct attention of most of the world. Even the U.N. had authorized sanctions against the country.

With the latest change in leadership in the country at the end of 2011, the threats only amplified. The new leader, Kim Jong-un, wanted to maintain full control over its citizens. Guidance from China and Russia was becoming a nuisance. Threats from Russia to cut off support to North Korea if they didn't start paying off their debts were not met with exuberance by the North Korean leader.

For a country with only a military led industry, and limited economy, the leadership had turned to other ways of obtaining monetary resources.

It was one of those ways, which had disturbed the U.S. The U.S. was shocked to realize that North Korea was printing U.S. dollars.

The practice began all the way back in the 1970's, as one of their ways of disrupting the western economy. North Korea quickly learned how to manufacturer U.S. currency. $100 bills became the denomination of choice.

It was easy to pass fake bills in Asia, as the U.S. dollar was the currency of choice because of its stability.

Counterfeiting money is not an easy task. It was once thought that a good black and white copier could make the counterfeit bills. Once color copiers became available, they could continue to make the phony bills even when countries tried to make it harder by using high cost color inks.

However, in an effort to pass the bills through banks, the bogus bills had to pass the security measures that countries were building into their bank notes, including a watermark, which was difficult to reproduce.

The U.S. currency has many safe measures built into it to prevent such fakes from circulation. It is printed on a special paper – made up of a combination of three-quarters cotton and one-quarter linen fibers. The printing comes from a highly specialized plate that has been hand engraved to such detail that only a few people in the world could copy it. There is even a security thread that can be picked up by the scanners at banks to spot any fakes.

In addition, the U.S. dollar is printed by the U.S. Bureau of Engraving and Printing on intaglio printing presses, which cost over five million dollars each.

Several major countries use the same type of printing press to produce their currency to prevent would be counterfeiters from destroying their economy.

Therein lies the problem.

With the death of his father, Kim Jong-sung, and the later, the default of the nation's loans in the 1970's, the new leader of North Korea at the time, Kim Jong-il, used the fake money to run his economy. His predecessor, Kim Jong-sung, had started the operations to reproduce foreign currency. With the assistance of Russia, the money was spread through many countries.

However, it was in the 1980's, that the U.S. became concerned. Under their new leader Kim Jong-il, the quality of the fake bills improved and was almost as good as the real U.S. bills. Counterfeit dollars were becoming harder to detect and were being spread throughout the world.

In Belfast, the Irish Republican Army was responsible for distributing fake U.S. dollars in Ireland and in Great Brittan.

At least forty-five million dollars of fake United States currency was put into circulation. Most of it was in fifty and one hundred-dollar denominations. All of which were printed in North Korea. And, it was only the start.

To protect their currencies from counterfeits, many of the world's nations realized they had to improve their methods of printing. Colors were used. In fact, on some bills, the colors changed as the angle of the light changed. In addition, much more detail was set into the engraving. It definitely made it harder for counterfeiters. The U.S. hoped that the changes would make passing counterfeit North Korean dollars almost impossible to pass through the banking system.

Unfortunately, it didn't take North Korea very long to copy the new currency. They were so good that the U.S. Secret Service called them "super notes."

In a large sting operation in 2005, Sean Garland - the president of the Irish Workers' Party was arrested for using counterfeit money. The arrest led to sanctions being slapped on a bank in Macau that was suspected of money laundering.

It appeared that he had been obtaining the bogus bills in Russia. Russia had become the broker for the counterfeit U.S. dollars produced in North Korea. Pressure was put on Moscow to stop the illegal trade of counterfeit bills.

The sting was followed by a sham wedding ceremony on a New Jersey yacht. The occasion on the yacht brought together additional smugglers of fake bills into a trap. Once they were rounded up, the sting led Treasury Agents to almost $67,000 in counterfeit bills stored in a locker at Moscow's Railway Station.

North Korea was selling the currency for twenty-five to fifty cents on the dollar to organizations that would use the remaining profit to run their illegal programs.

Once again, the U.S. dollar had to make some revisions to make it more difficult to counterfeit.

The largest sting involved Customs officials who were attempting to stop illegal cigarettes from being shipped into the United States in yet another attempt to obtain U.S. dollars by North Korea.

To the surprise of FBI Special Agent Bob Harner, who was in on the cigarette sting, they were offered high-quality counterfeit currency to distribute in addition to the cigarettes. The operation bagged $4.5 million dollars in counterfeit currency and resulted in 87 indictments against suspects ranging from the U.S., Canada, Taiwan, and China.

This took the currency people in the Secret Service by surprise. The operations by North Korea were far more extensive than they realized. The other problem was that the bills were better than the U.S. originals. Someone had improved on the original printing plate's intentional defects.

The stings in 2005 slowed down the counterfeits from North Korea. Or, at least that's what the U.S. hoped.

To replace the sale of fake U.S. dollars, North Korea turned to drug trafficking throughout Japan and Asia, insurance scams, and recently, computer frauds.

Additional changes in 2009, made the U.S. dollars almost impossible to reproduce. Benjamin Franklin's portrait has become one of the most familiar portraits in world currency.

Anyone attempting to reproduce the bills were usually identified once any quantity tried passing the tests at world banks. Treasury and Secret Service Agents spent countless hours mapping out the locations where small quantities of easily identifiable bills were being passed. Many small-time counterfeiters were stopped.

Once more, in 2013, the U.S. redesigned the $100 bill, adding two new, advanced anti-counterfeiting features: a woven 3D ribbon that scrolls when the bill is tilted, and a color-changing image of a bell.

Treasury officials were the first to point out how difficult it would be to counterfeit the new bills.

Recently, appliances, which were a luxury in North Korea and very difficult to obtain, were shipped over the border and presented to North Korea's new leader Kim Jong-un and his supporters. You guessed it; they were purchased using new bogus U.S. bills.

It appeared North Korea was back in business.

When you add in the nuclear threats to South Korea, Japan and the United States, along with drug and computer frauds, North

Korea has become a thorn in the U.S.'s side. Even Russia was backing off supporting North Korea activates. World pressure was starting to mount.

The final straw was made when North Korea got greedy enough to use their dirty tricks on China, who had been selling goods to them to keep their nation from starving.

Counterfeit Chinese dollars were starting to show up in the payments for these goods. Desperate for finances, North Korea had turned on the country that was feeding it.

That last straw had fallen hard. A North Korean agent was arrested in a border city after exchanging five million dollars for Chinese currency at two banks in Dandong China, and then depositing the funds. The recent exchange of funds was reported in the South Korean JoongAng Daily, which further embarrassed the Chinese government.

For many years, the organization in North Korea charged with making the counterfeit currency was known as Room 39. It was actually started back in the 1970's by Kim Jong-sung. When his son Kim Jong-il became the Supreme Chairman of North Korea, the program was increased.

The location of Room 39 has been kept secret over the years. Rumors have located it in several locations; however, the CIA has never been able to confirm its location.

With the death of Kim Jong-il, his son Kim Jong-un has only stepped up the ratchet on illegal activates against the world's economy in order to finance his own military led economy.

A recent report to congress stated; North Korea's economy is only one disaster away from complete collapse.

For years, the CIA had heard that the blueprints to the secret buildings of North Korea were stored somewhere in the many rooms of the Grand People's Study House. Perhaps room 39 could be found.

If the printing presses could be located and stopped, and perhaps the location of the cyberwarfare could be located, eliminating one or both of them might be the final nail that could have the effect of bringing the country to its knees and force out its leaders.

If it did, it could put a stop to their nuclear program.

Compared to the risk of all-out war to stop their nuclear and missile programs, it might be the only way to bring about change. Thus, the CIA proposed a program, indicating that it would be worth a shot to see if U.S. and China negotiators could use the Chen-Lee Tea Company in Hong Kong to bargain with the smugglers to get the important blueprints out of North Korea.

In order to convince someone to take the huge risk involved in looking for the blueprints, United States and Chinese authorities needed to increase the bait that might get someone in North Korea to smuggle the drawings out, if they could be found.

The decision was made; a currier of the Chen-Lee Tea Company would be the carrier of the resulting offer to North Korea.

Pyongyang North Korea

Jung Chang-Sun had made a couple trips to the Chinese border to pick up food supplies. He was one of the drivers of a three-truck convoy that made the trip a couple times a week.

He hoped his contact would be there to discuss the list he supplied to them during their last transaction. Now, he was becoming concerned that no one had contacted him in the last two trips.

Had they rejected the other items in the Grand People's Study House? The drawings and paintings were extremely valuable. He doubted that the smugglers couldn't find a buyer for the artifacts. Perhaps it was his demand for a higher price.

As he approached the warehouse just over the border into China, he spotted his contact working at the loading dock. While the truck was being loaded, the contact took him aside and asked him if he wanted a cigarette. Jung Chang-Sun did not smoke. He could not afford the habit in North Korea. Therefore, he brushed off the offer.

"Take the smokes," his contact told him in a firm voice.

Jung Chang-Sun realized there might have been a message in the pack and quickly put it in his pocket.

When he turned around, his contact was walking away. It was a short meeting and Jung Chang-Sun wondered what sort of message had been placed in the pack of cigarettes.

Now, his only chance was to wait until the caravan of trucks were safely on the road back to North Korea to look. He could not risk any chances of having anyone see him take a message out of the cigarettes. He wondered if the offers for the items they had listed were indeed big enough for the risks they were taking.

Like his friend Duri Sol Ju, he was worried about the dangers the smuggling operation carried to his family.

Jung Chang-Sun was half way to the border when he was brave enough to open the pack of cigarettes. Inside, he found a very thin silk note folded around the cigarettes. He slipped it out to read it as he drove.

It was not what he expected.

He glanced at the thin page, folded it up and slipped it under his shirt near his waist. His belt would help hold it in place. It would remain there until he was safely back home.

At the border, he was extremely nervous while the guards did their normal inspection. When he and the other trucks were waved on, his heart rate started to beat normally, once again.

Arriving at the warehouse, his boss asked him if the trip went okay. Jung Chang-Sun told his boss it went okay and offered him the pack of cigarettes some Chinese dockworker had left in the back of the truck when he was loading the supplies.

"I do not smoke," he informed him. "You can have them."

It was a big gift in North Korea and his boss put him in high favor for it.

When Jung Chang-Sun arrived home, he went to a quiet spot in his small house and carefully read the note. He did not want his family to see it.

The note was written in very small print. It stated that they were interested in one more item. They wanted a blueprint for a building. The blueprint was rumored to be stored in the sub-basement of the Grand People's Study House.

The payment for the item would be a way out of North Korea for him and his family. It would be arranged. If he agreed, he should turn his lights on when he arrived at the warehouse on his next trip. Further information would then be supplied.

Jung Chang-Sun put the note in the stove and burned it.

The next day, he met Duri So Ju on his way home from the Grand People's Study House.

"We have a problem," he told him. "They did not offer us money for any of the items on the list."

"Why?" Duri Sol Ju asked. "Are they not good enough?"

"They made a request and an offer. We need to talk in a quiet place. Meet me in the Kim Il-sung Square in an hour," he suggested, knowing that the square would be dark and empty of people at that hour. It would make it easier to spot anyone trying to listen in on their conversation.

Chapter 31

Decisions

An hour later, a very nervous Duri Sol Ju met Jung Chang-Sun at the park.

"Tell me, why did they reject the list we gave them? You know how hard it is to get something out of the building. I cannot take anything bigger or something like a statue."

Jung Chang-Sun told him about the note he was given at the warehouse in China.

"Duri, they want a blueprint of a building. They say it is kept in the Grand People's Study House. They say they will get me and my family out of the country if I can get it for them.

"Can you find it? What should I tell them? If we don't do it, they may tell the authorities that we have smuggled two drawings out of the country."

Duri Sol Ju asked, "What about me and my family? I am taking all the risk. What if they catch me?"

"I can tell them it is both our families or nothing," Jung Chang-Sun replied. "They must want it very badly. They will pay for it by getting both of us out of North Korea.

"Duri, can you find what they are looking for?"

"What is it?"

"I do not know. They said they would tell me on the next trip if we agreed. What should I do?"

"When is your next trip?" Duri Sol Ju asked.

"Two days. We have two days to decide if we will do it or not."

"Good. Let me see if I can find out if blueprints are indeed kept in the building. Then, if I find them, I will see if there is a way to get one out. Until then, say nothing."

The two men silently went back home, concerned about the prospects of their conversation.

The risks were going up. However, the risk of several more drawings taken out of the room might be just as high.

The contact offered a way out of North Korea. It was what they were hoping for with all the smuggling. Could the two of them do it? Could they really get both families out of North Korea at the same time? What kind of risk would that involve? What if the Bowibu found out?

Perhaps their contact would take the blueprint and drown the families at sea? Could they be trusted with their lives? Then again, could the new leader of North Korea be trusted? People were starving and because there was no heat, they were freezing.

The next two days seemed as if it took a year. This was not an easy decision.

At the end of the next day, Duri Sol Ju met with Jung Chang-Sun away from their houses.

"I think I have found a room that contains the blueprints to many buildings," he informed Jung Chang-Sun. The person that cleans in there is someone I know. If we pay him well, I think we can get him to hand one over to me. He hates his job and wants out. He has told me so in the past."

"Can he be trusted?" Jung Chang-Sun asked.

"We can see once you get the information on what they are looking for.

"Remember, it is both of our families or nothing. We must stick to that. I do not want to go back for more."

"I understand. I will tell them tomorrow."

Now, the burden was on Jung Chang-Sun. Could he convince his contacts to help both families out of North Korea? It was a huge price to be paid.

When it was Jung Chang-Sun's day to travel to China, he was very nervous. Was it a trap? Perhaps someone had been tipped off and they would be looking for someone with their lights on.

How could he convince them that they needed to get two families out of North Korea? What if someone overheard their conversation? What blueprint was so important that they would approach them to smuggle it out? Could they get a large print out of the building and then out of the country?

If someone wanted it that bad, they must have thought about a way it could be removed.

He passed the border and headed for the warehouse. As he pulled his truck into the parking area, he turned his lights on.

A couple minutes later, a man banged on his door. "Turn your lights out," he shouted.

When he was pulling the truck up to the loading dock, he spotted his usual contact. He was bringing crates of food out to the truck.

They met at the side of the truck. "Meet me inside, he told Jung Chang-Sun.

Jung Chang-Sun waited a minute and then walked into the warehouse. Inside, the contact handed Jung Chang-Sun a piece of paper with two places on it – Room 39 and the Cyberwarfare Room.

He told Jung Chang-Sun that he needed at least one of the blueprints. With that, he handed him a mini-camera to take a picture of the blueprint. "When you get the photo, take the memory chip out by pressing here, and destroy the camera," he instructed him. "The camera is made of plastic so it will not be detected by metal detectors."

Jung Chang-Sun balked at taking the camera. "I have a helper. We need to get both of our families out of North Korea. This is very risky. You know what will happen if the secret police catch us."

The man thought about it for a minute. "Okay, but you will have to get both blueprints and their locations."

"How do I let you know when we have them?" he asked.

"Put a red piece of paper by your door. Someone will contact you."

"When will we get out?" he asked.

"When you have the prints on the chip. Don't lose it. It is your pass to get out of North Korea. Stay quiet and do not let anyone know what you are doing or you will never see your family again. You know the risks. Do it as quickly as you can.

With that, Jung Chang-Sun took the camera and hid the list of buildings along with the mini-camera in his pants.

When his truck was loaded, he got in and drove it, along with the other trucks, back towards the border.

Once on the road, he took the camera out of his pants and tucked it under the dashboard of the truck, above the steering column. He left the list tucked into the inside his pants.

At the border crossing, the inspection of his truck went without incidents. After inspecting his cargo for contraband, he was waved on.

Pulling into his warehouse, his boss met him at the truck. "You get any cigarettes?" he asked.

"No, they didn't leave any in my truck on this trip," he answered. His boss sighed and walked away.

Then, Jung Chang-Sun reached under the dashboard, and removed the camera, placing it back in his pants.

As Jung Chang-Sun was heading home from the warehouse, Duri Sol Ju was waiting for him on the route he always took walking home.

"Meet me in the square in one hour," Jung Chang-Sun told him as they passed each other.

Duri Sol Ju gave him a nod, and kept on walking without making further eye contact.

An hour later, found the two of them alone in the Kim Il-sung Square. They took a walk down the middle of the square and back. During that time, they made sure no one was watching them as they talked.

"Duri, they agreed to take both of us and our families. However, they need two blueprints and their locations. Think you can do it?"

"I do not know. How can I get a big blueprint out of the building without being noticed?"

"They gave me a camera. All they want is the memory chip that is inside of the camera." Jung Chang-Sun showed Duri Sol Ju where it was, and how it could be removed. It was extremely small. It would be easy to conceal.

"How am I to get the camera in without being caught?" he asked.

"It is all plastic. It will not set off the metal detector and no one is looking for anyone bringing something small into the building. They are looking for people taking things out. Think you can do it?"

Duri Sol Ju looked at the two places on the list. Room 39 and the Cyberwarfare Room would not be easy to find. He had heard rumors about them. However, he had never seen either of them.

At least, with the camera, he didn't need to worry about copying a blueprint by hand or trying to remove it from the building.

Duri was worried about trusting his co-worker. However, if the price was right, he felt that he would help, provided that he was not involved after he took the pictures. Once Duri Sol Ju found the blueprints, his co-worker would be paid and their involvement would end. That would be it, no further contact.

Jung Chang-Sun told him how he was to place a piece of red paper near the door when they had the prints.

"They said someone will contact us. Duri, they must have someone in North Korea. If they want the chip, we will have to make sure they get us out first."

Duri nodded his head, and told Jung Chang-Sun that he would make an attempt to find them.

Then, they headed home, separately; making sure once again that no one was watching or following them.

Chapter 32

The Plea

FBI Agent Mark Lawson

As the sting was sprung on the "organization," I decided to give our suspect up in Superior, Wisconsin one more shot at revealing his information, before he hit the courts.

In the morning, I contacted Sheriff Bernaski and suggested that before he was forced to turn his prisoner over to Federal custody, that the two of us should take one more shot at seeing what information we could get out of him. There was still the matter of the shooting, where his gun was used in the past. We had a direct match on the shooting but little information about it. We might be able to use it to get some additional information from him.

Later that day, I drove up to Superior from Minneapolis and met with Sheriff Bernaski and our suspect.

The suspect was not in a very cooperative mood. Considering the seriousness of the crime he committed, I couldn't blame him. He was looking at life in prison for the killing of a Customs agent.

As far as our suspect was concerned, the less cooperative he was, the better off he would have it once he was committed to the inside of the prison. At this point, he had reached the realization that the Fed's had the goods on him.

I think Sheriff Bernaski and I caught him by surprise when we told our suspect that he was going be charged on Federal smuggling charges, in addition to first degree murder, and attempting to shoot an endangered animal out of season.

The last charge was the least of his worries.

"So, you going to add an extra thirty years to my life sentence?" he asked.

"You want to try and get out at age 120?" I replied. That's a long time to be stuck in a place like Leavenworth. Ever been in solitary confinement? You'll be lucky to get out of your cell for the first three to five years. After a while, listening to your own breath is the most important thing in your life. There is nothing else."

"So, what do you have to offer?" he asked me. "As an FBI Agent, you didn't drive all the way up here from Minneapolis to see what I looked like, did you?"

I paused for a full two minutes as I wanted to let the realizations sink in to his mind.

"Perhaps you could tell us something about the operations of the "organization" and how they contacted you," I suggested. "You may not get out of the charges, but if you cooperate, we might be able to get you placed in a better location. You probably don't want to be down in the deep south without air conditioning, do you? For someone that lives up north, it is hard to adjust.

"A good word from the FBI can go a long way with the judge and the prison system," I told him.

"That the best you can offer?" he asked.

"You got something or not?" I asked.

Over the next hour, the suspect slowly started to give up some of his best-kept secrets. He was not going to escape the murder case.   It was obvious, and he knew it. If he could get some benefits for providing some information, he was willing to give us the clues.

"You know about the "organization?" the subject asked. "I've only had a few dealings with them in the past few years. It was mainly protection. They wanted to make sure that no one got too close to their people. I was, as they say, paid security. I was paid to watch and make sure there was no surveillance of their operations.

"Unfortunately, your Customs man got too close and I was requested to eliminate him."

"Who gave you that order?" I asked.

He gave me the name of a man in Toronto that was his main contact.

After talking a little more about the Toronto operation, I told him that I needed a little more information if I was going to help him out.

He offered up one more bit of information that caught us by surprise.

As we both listened, the suspect told us that he taped all of his conversations with the "organization."

"The geniuses gave me a burner phone to protect themselves from being traced, he said. "I guess they never heard of an app that allows you to record a conversation. I got most of my orders by text message. However, every once in a while I needed to talk to them to make sure about the details of the operation. I have them all recorded."

I sat back in my chair, "That would definitely make murder charges for the individuals in Toronto easier to enforce. "So, what information do the recordings offer?" I asked.

"They told me about the guy killed up in Two Harbors when they were trying to make a diversion. You got info on that one?" he asked me.

If he actually had that on tape, we might be able to arrest someone on charges of manslaughter for the accidental killing of the seaman from the Calvin Wroth.

That one caught my attention.

Later that afternoon, Sheriff Bernaski and I accompanied the suspect to the suspect's farmhouse.

High up in the rafters of his shed he had hid a coffee can containing a hard drive with audio and text files from the "organization."

Since they had been copied from one electronic device to another, the courts would have to decide their relevance. However, for our case in Two Harbors, we had the smoking gun. Now, we could push the dockworkers buttons, and see if we could get a confession.

I called Deputy Alex North and told her the story. She told me she would track the man down that dropped the bucket.

The suspect was back in his cozy cell by dinnertime. I made sure he got a good dessert from the local restaurant. I think he got my message.

Then, I made a call to contact Customs in New Jersey. I gave them the good news about the information of the hard drive. They were eager to get their hands on the messages and asked that we transmit the data to them as quickly as possible. The original would be locked up as evidence.

With the closing of the ore dock for winter, our suspect in Two Harbors skipped town. He didn't even stay on for the final couple of weeks of winter maintenance on the conveyor line.

Deputy North put out a bulletin on him, and had his credit cards monitored.

The credit trail pointed to a small town in Oregon. She sent me a message, and asked that the FBI contact the local police for picking up our suspect.

It only took one day to locate him and have him arrested. When the Police Chief there contacted me, I told her about the messages we obtained from our murder suspect. I asked her to accidentally mention the messages to her suspect in jail.

"I was hoping that if he knew we had this evidence, he might be willing to talk."

About two hours later, I got a call from the Police Chief.

"Agent Lawson, you want to join me in Las Vegas? With your luck, I want you to spin the roulette wheel for me.

"When I told your man that you had evidence on tape, from some boss in Toronto, that he had killed someone, he turned white. A few minutes later, he was singing like a bird. When do you want to pick him up? He's already waived extradition from Oregon."

"I guess I'll owe you one. I'll have the Marshall's office send someone to pick him up, and have him delivered into Federal custody.

It was indeed our lucky day. I called Deputy North and let her know that her case appeared to have been solved, and we had her suspect in custody.

We had a good conversation, and once again, I asked her if she was interested in an FBI position. She would make a good agent.

Two days later, the Two Harbor's suspect was back in Minnesota, in the Duluth jail, awaiting charges for manslaughter.

Later, Deputy Alex North was given a commendation for the work done in capturing the two murder suspects in the case.

Two weeks later, FBI Special Agent Mark Lawson received a letter in his basket. It was an application for employment in the FBI, addressed from Alex North.

Chapter 33

The Search

Pyongyang North Korea

Jung Chang-Sun and his friend Duri Sol Ju had a tough task. They had to locate two buildings in ultra-high security areas, as well as find the blueprints for them located in a concealed room deep in the Grand People's Study House without anyone finding out what they were doing. It was definitely a task of desperation on their part.

While Duri Sol Ju was taking most of the risk trying to find a blueprint in a room he was not authorized to maintain, Jung Chang-Sun was trying to find people he trusted to find out if any of them knew about the existence of a place called Room 39.

The excuse he used for talking about Room 39 was that he saw the money that was paid to the Chinese warehouse for food supplies. It was crisp new bills. He had heard long ago about the government printing Chinese money. Now, he wondered where and how it was done. How could they make money so perfect that the Chinese would accept it?

He knew there was a risk in asking people. If the wrong person heard the request, he would be immediately placed under surveillance by the government.

At the same time, Duri Sol Ju took considerable caution in approaching his friend at work. The question running through his mind was at what price his friend would be willing to take the risk of letting Duri see the blueprints, that is, if they even existed.

His hope was that, as in the huge room he worked, everything was placed on a log sheet. If the places were in the log, they could quickly find them, and he could be out of the room in very little time. If not, he had to hope that his friend knew exactly where to look.

Both Duri and Jung Chang-Sun knew that it would be easier if they knew where the buildings were located first.

As Duri Sol Ju left work that day, he waited until his co-worker came out of the building. Then, he walked up to him.

"Can we meet somewhere and talk?" he asked. "I have a problem, and I'm hoping you can give me a suggestion of how to handle it."

It was a simple request. It was one that offered no hint as to the severity of the request.

Later, the two men met at an open area where they might be free to talk without others listening to their conversation.

Duri Sol Ju approached the man with the request. "I know you don't like working for the government, maintaining a room that does not exist. I have a favor to ask. I would like to see a blueprint of a building that might be in your files.

"I know there are risks. I could pay you for it."

His co-worker looked shocked. He had never had anyone ask him to risk his job, let alone his life, for money.

"What building and how much?" he quietly asked, while looking around to see who might be watching.

"Are you willing to look?" Duri asked.

"Perhaps! If the price is worth the risk. How much?"

It was a good sign. Perhaps, things were open for bargaining with his co-worker. Unfortunately, Duri Sol Ju had no idea as to a starting price to offer.

"I would be willing to offer you a year's pay to look at the blueprint. That's 65,000 Won - KPW, (about $840.00 U.S.)."

"That's a lot of money for a look at a blueprint. What's it for?" he asked.

"Room 39. Do we have a deal?"

"Why do you want that?" he asked.

"I think our government is printing Chinese money as well as U.S. dollars. I want to find the location and determine if I could buy some at a discount. I want to pass the money off to Chinese merchants. If you help, I might be able to bring you in on a deal to get some merchandise at a reduced price."

"And if we get caught?" he answered. Who's going to save us from getting shot?"

"How are they going to catch us for looking?" Duri Sol Ju asked. "That's your job, maintaining the items in the room. You just allowed me in because I had a question on handling thin papers like they stored in your area, to make sure they did not get ruined."

His co-worker thought it through. "How long would it take?"

"If you have it in your log, perhaps five, maybe ten minutes. Then, I'm out of there and you have your money."

"Let me look tomorrow. If you know where the building is, it would be easier."

They split company and did not meet up until after work the following day. It was a cold day and the first of the winter storms had moved in.

Duri Sol Ju met him as he left work. With the cold, everyone was bundled up in their winter wear as they walked home.

"Any news?" he asked.

"Not on the list," he answered. "You'll need a location for me to find it. Too bad, I could have used the money."

"I have another building. Can you check on the Cyberwarfare Building?"

"That's high-security, it will cost you more."

Duri Sol Ju was pleased that he hadn't rejected the thought of another location. A higher price could be met. He was still hoping that Jung Chang-Sun could come up with a location for Room 39. If he did, they could search for the building where it was located.

That evening, Jung Chang-Sun stopped by Duri Sol Ju's house. They went out for a short walk.

Duri Sol Ju filled Jung Chang-Sun in on the conversations with his co-worker.

"So far, I feel that he can be trusted. He definitely wants the money. I told him I was looking to get a deal with the Chinese merchants, using some discounted counterfeit bills. I also told him that I would let him in on the deal if I found the source of money.

"Unfortunately, he told me that Room 39 was not on his list. That means either it is in another building on the list, or the blueprints may not be in his room.

"We'll have to try other ways to locate it.

"When he mentioned that he was looking forward to the extra money, I asked about the Cyberwarfare Building. He told me he would look at the list tomorrow. It would cost us additional money."

"Duri, I might have found a lead on Room 39. I talked to another friend that thought he had a friend that brought supplies to Room 39. It was cotton and linen shreds. He thought it might be for making some kind of special paper.

"My friend told me he would get back to me tomorrow and let me know if he was correct. If he is right, we may have that lead we need.

"Duri, keep your co-worker close. If we can get both of the blueprints, we might be looking at a warmer climate in a week or two. Don't give up hope. You can do it."

They parted company and headed back to their homes. Now, they realized that there was at least a glimmer of hope that they might be able to pull it off.

The next day, the sun was shining. It was a good omen.

By the end of the day, Duri Sol Ju had talked to his co-worker and he had located the blueprint on his log. It was in the files. He had not pulled it out to inspect it, so if they did it the next day, he could say it was simply out for cleaning if anyone walked in on them.

Just before he reached his house, Duri saw his friend Jung Chang-Sun waiting at a corner for him.

As he approached him, Jung Chang-Sun told him, "Good news, Duri. My friend gave me a location for Room 39.

"Now I know why he didn't see it on the log. It appears that Room 39 is hidden in a supply ship in the harbor. From what I'm told, it rarely leaves the harbor, except for a short trip into open waters once a year when the Supreme Chairman inspects the fleet."

He handed Duri the ships number. "You think they are listed in the room just like the buildings?"

"I can find out tomorrow. I'll bring the camera," Duri informed him. "Wish me luck. If I need more money, I'll let you know.

"You think they will take both our families, if we only have the location of the one of their targets?"

"Have faith," Jung Chang-Sun replied. "Tomorrow looks like a sunny day. Be careful. Think warm climates."

When Duri Sol Ju reported for work the next day, he worked in his concealed room for two hours before locking it up and knocking on the door of his co-workers room.

As he answered the door, he looked both ways for anyone observing them and quickly pulled Duri into the room.

"Are you absolutely sure no one saw you leaving your room and heading this way?" he inquired.

"I was careful. Where's the blueprint?"

They walked to the back corner of the room and opened a file drawer labeled 236. Inside were the blueprints to ten buildings.

"Which one is it?" Duri Sol Ju asked.

His co-worker pulled out the third one from the bottom. "This one."

He laid it on the top of the others, while Duri Sol Ju took out his camera.

"You didn't tell me you were going to take picture. What if someone catches us? What will we do?" his co-worker asked.

"Relax. In a few minutes, we will be done and you will have your money. They will never find the camera, I promise you. Do you have the blueprints for Navy vessels? I heard last night that Room 39 might be located in a Navy supply ship. I have the number."

"No, only the buildings. When do I get my money?"

"I can meet you tonight. I'll have your money," I explained to him.

"I need more money for that building. I want 80,000 Won. You made more risk using the camera."

"Well, you didn't want me to make a paper copy of the blueprint in your room did you? It would have been too big for me to take out of the building. The camera was the best choice. I'll have the 80,000 Won for you tonight, just as I promised."

They arranged for a meeting place.

Duri Sol Ju left the blueprint room and headed back to his assigned room. So far, he had not seen anyone in the hallways. It was expected that it would be that way. Except to throw cleaning supplies in the trash, everyone was normally in their assigned rooms until it was time to leave at the end of the day. Discussions with other workers were extremely rare and not approved.

When he reached his room, he unlocked his door and made sure no one had seen him in the hall. Then, he carefully removed the memory chip from the camera. It was about one centimeter by one centimeter. It was easily hidden in the torn seam of his coat.

Once the chip was hidden, he stashed the camera inside a Tang Dynasty vase. Depending on how diligent his replacement might be, once Duri was safely out of North Korea, it would take a minimum of a year before the vase was on the list for cleaning. Usually, they only dusted the outside. Since no one else ever entered the room, it might be there for another thousand years.

At the end of the day, Duri grabbed his heavy wool winter jacket and headed up the many steps to the security station.

After the usual quick inspection of his pockets, the guard waved him on.

As Duri left the building, his knees almost buckled. He had done the impossible. Now, after paying his co-worker later that evening, he would tell Jung Chang-Sun that he could put the piece of red paper near his door.

Even with all the cards falling in place, Jung Chang-Sun didn't dare tell his family or pack anything including extra money. They still had the concern of being caught before they got out of the country. The slightest slip of the tongue could mean disaster to the family.

Chapter 34

Payments

That evening, Duri Sol Ju met with his co-worker in the Kim Il-sung Square, which was between the Grand People's Study House and the Taedong River.

He thanked him for his help and handed him the 80,000 Won they had agreed upon for payment.

"I'm not going to ask what you are going to do with the picture. Let's just say we never met and leave it at that," his co-worker told him. "I don't want to have problems with the Bowibu (the secret police)."

Then, without shaking hands, they parted.

The next morning, Jung Chang-Sun put a small piece of red paper on top of the door trim of his house. It looked as if the wind had caught a piece of paper and blown it up above the door.

When Duri Sol Ju arrived at work, it was maintenance as usual. He did not arrive at security at the same time as his co-worker, and that was fine with him.

For Duri, it was simply another day of cleaning and maintaining the extremely old artifacts stored in his room.

At the end of the workday, he had an extra spring to his legs as he climbed the steps, went through security, and exited the building.

Temporarily, he felt the pressure was off. Now, he needed to wait for directions on how someone was going to get them safely out of North Korea.

The piece of paper stayed on the top of the door for three days without a response. Jung Chang-Sun was becoming concerned. Surely, if someone wanted the blueprints, they would come to find them. He wondered if his new contacts were simply extremely cautious. Perhaps someone wasn't watching the door. On the other hand, perhaps they were making sure there were no government workers laying a trap.

Even Duri Sol Ju was becoming concerned. He took some extreme risks to take the picture. Where were they? They should have responded by now.

On the fourth day, as Jung Chang-Sun was returning from work, he was met by a man in the street he did not know.

"You have something for me?" he asked.

Jung Chang-Sun turned and looked at him. "Yes! When can we meet?"

"Tomorrow. Meet me at the market after work. We'll find a place we can talk."

"Can my friend come too? He took the picture."

"Too many people. Just you and me. I don't want to draw attention," he instructed me. "Don't be late."

Then he was gone.

Jung thought, *"Fortunately, it is not my day to go to China. I will be available after work to meet with him and not worry about any delays at the border."*

Duri Sol Ju met with me as he was heading home.

"Duri, they made contact. They want to meet with just me, tomorrow, to discuss plans. I have a good feeling about it. I think we may finally be about to leave."

Duri Sol Ju was pleased to hear that they finally made contact. In addition, he understood why they did not want more than one person to talk to. When several people gather in public, people pay attention. It was the last thing they needed.

Duri Sol Ju told him, "Make sure you tell them that they get the picture after we are out of the country. It is our only guarantee that they will follow up on their side of the bargain.

"We took too much risk for them to get the prize and leave us empty-handed."

"I understand. I will talk to you tomorrow after I meet with them."

"Also, don't tell your family. We must keep this secret. Our lives depend on it. Come to my place and we can go for a walk. I don't want anyone including my family to hear our plans. There will be a time to let them know."

"Duri, I do understand. Trust me. I'll see you tomorrow. We'll have it all worked out."

Now we were both filled with nervous anticipation. How soon will we be able to leave? How will they get us out?

The next day, I had a hard time keeping from thinking about my meeting. I was sure that Duri was having the same thoughts.

It must be by boat. That was the only way I could think of getting out.

The question was; how would they do it? How could they keep us from being caught? The waters were heavily patrolled. Would we leave late at night? Would they be traveling with us, or just hide us on a boat?

Any thought of climbing over the mountains in the winter was not a good idea. Besides, the military had guards and mines all over the mountain passes. And then, there was the fence at the Demilitarize Zone. How could you get through? Did they have a secret tunnel? It was rumored that the military had tunnels all over the hills so they could invade South Korea, someday.

Yes, this was a good time to get out of North Korea. There was too much military tension. One slip by the Supreme Chairman and there could be war.

Jung Chang-Sun definitely wanted his family out and safe. The thoughts of what obstacles might be waiting in a start-over of a new life had not even occurred to him.

At the end of the workday, Jung Chang-Sun went directly to the market, which was close to his warehouse. Most of the items sold at the market came from his warehouse, so he was very familiar with it.

He walked the rows between the street vendors looking for his contact. So far, people were just starting to appear at the market as they left work.

As the crowd was starting to grow, he spotted him. He was standing off to the side of the market. Slowly, after they made eye contact, he started heading Jung Chang-Sun's way.

Jung Chang-Sun held his breath for a split second. This was it...

The man motioned for him to come and join him.

Jung Chang-Sun slowly walked that way. He didn't want to draw anyone's attention as he made his way to his contact.

When he reached the man, the two of them turned and slowly started walking towards a narrow street that led away from the market. It was a long narrow street with very few people in the street.

When they reached what appeared to be a safe place to talk, his contact asked, "Did you bring the chip?"

"No, I will have it with me when you get all us out of North Korea. How will you do it?"

"Did you get both prints?" he asked.

"No, the one does not have a blueprint. However, I have a location for both. It is the best we could do. You have not answered my question. How will you get us out and when? The longer we wait, the more dangerous it gets. It is hard to keep secrets."

"Did you tell anyone?" he asked.

"No. Only Duri So Ju. Even our families do not know."

"Good. Tell no one," the man reminded me.

"So, tell me. What comes next? I need to know."

After checking to make sure no one was within listening range, my contact told me the plan.

"It will happen in three days, when there is a scheduled demonstration for the government in the Kim Il-sung Square. Everyone will be there to show their support for the Supreme Chairman. He will make an appearance there as well.

"It is planned for 1:00 pm in the afternoon.

"When everyone is cleaning up Kim Il-sung Square for the demonstration, you will head to the Taedong River. You and your families need to be at the place just before where the river splits and then comes back together. It is just before the Haebangsan Street Bridge.

"At the end of the park, on the river, there is a dock on the west side of the river. Stay near the trees in separate groups until you see me at the dock.

"A river barge will pick you up at that dock at noon. Make sure you are there. It will not wait.

"When I give you the sign, you and your families walk out slowly, a couple people at a time. We don't want to draw attention. Talk quietly as though you are enjoying the walk along the river.

"Do not bring anything other than the clothes you will be wearing. You don't want to draw any attention.

"Most of the town will be heading for the square.

"There may be police watching the area around the square. My hope is that all the police will be heading for the square to march with all the others. It is our best chance to leave without drawing a lot of attention."

"Wouldn't it be safer at night?" I asked.

"No, they watch the river closely at night. Middle of the day is the best time to leave, right in full sight.

"We will hide you inside the barge. They will not stop us. I have taken care of it. Our biggest risk is out in the ocean.

"Our papers show the barge is bringing boxes to China, returning with supplies. I have taken care of the river patrols. Unfortunately, the Navy may stop us. If they do, you must stay silent."

"You think they will?" I asked nervously.

"No. They see our barge every couple days. They usually just wave at us. They are looking for high-speed boats or submarines. Usually, it is all for show to make it look like we have a tough Navy. I doubt our boats could repel any real attack. I guess that's why we have such a big army and guns mounted along the river entrance.

"Now, tell your friend everything I have told you. Just make sure you bring the information you gathered."

"Will you be on the boat?" I asked.

"Yes, they asked me to go with you to make sure you arrive safely. So, go there quietly, and do not make it look anything different than a family walk. May God go with you."

It caught me by surprise. I rarely heard anyone say that expression anymore. It was another reason I wanted my family out of North Korea. I was afraid my family would forget religion as many of the others here in North Korea have been brainwashed into doing.

I told him we would be there at the designated time. As we parted company, I wondered how we would get both of our families to the park without anyone wondering why we were heading away from the Kim Il-sung Square.

Even though it was cold outside, we needed to leave early. We could not afford any delays that would cause us to miss the barge.

Later that evening, I told Duri Sol Ju everything I was told. We agreed that we would not tell our families until that morning, until we were safely in the park near the river.

Chapter 35

Operation Blue

Washington DC.

CIA headquarters was closely monitoring the project out of North Korea. It was in the best interests of China to cooperate. However, past history showed that China tended to take care of Chinese interests first.

The CIA had stuck their neck out supporting an attempt to smuggle blueprints of a top-secret buildings out of North Korea. If things did not go as planned, the North Korean leader Kim Jong-un would have a field day showing the world how the U.S. was spying on his country, and planning to commit an act of war. All of this would justify his nuclear missile defense program.

With his personality, it was not a position that the U.S. wanted to be in.

Through CIA contacts in Hong Kong, including the offices of the Chen-Lee Tea Company, and government contacts in the

Chinese Capital of Beijing, the CIA maintained an hourly contact so that they could monitor the ongoing situation.

Everyone realized that the critical phase of the operation would fall on the day that the families were extracted from North Korea. However, with all the high-stakes poker games with North Korea, this operation was flagged with the code name of Operation Blue, and was given the same level of importance as monitoring the Russian activities in the Baltics.

The word that was received back in Washington was that the "information" was in hand.

However, until it was confirmed that the documents were safely out of the country, it was still a mystery to the CIA as to the whereabouts of the buildings.

Even the President was kept in the loop during his briefings.

Pyongyang North Korea

Three days was an extremely long time to wait when you are expecting to leave a country.

Both Jung Chang-Sun and Duri Sol Ju needed to keep their daily routine as normal as possible, so they went to work as normal. They were starting to realize that it would be the last two days they would be at their jobs.

Duri Sol Ju was becoming concerned about the camera he left in the vase, in the antiquities room of the People's Study House. If someone accidentally found it before he and his family was totally out of North Korea, everyone in North Korea would be looking for him.

When he got to work, he decided that since the camera was made of plastic, he would smash it into as many small pieces as he could. Then, he could put them in the trash buckets in the hall.

If he put a few pieces in several buckets, no one would be the wiser. The only pieces that he had to worry about were the lens and the camera's processor chip.

After thinking about the problem for an hour; in order to prevent anyone from hearing a loud crash, Duri Sol Ju put his jacket over the camera. Then, using a concrete stand used to display a statue, he crushed the camera under his coat. He struck it several times to make sure it was crushed.

Brushing off the pieces from his coat, all the camera's plastic pieces were under a centimeter in size. He ground the larger pieces one more time with the stand to make the pieces even smaller.

Perfect. He could put them in the trash without anyone knowing what they were from.

Even the lens shattered. He didn't realize that in a simple single lens camera, the lens is often made with a single piece of glass. With the solid blow made by the concrete stand, the glass lens shattered to what looked like pieces of dust.

Now, all he had to eliminate was the processor and the tiny battery. With the printed circuit on the composite material, the wafer thin square processor would have to be removed from the building.

It only took him a few moments to realize that the best place to hide it was in his shoe. When it came time to leave work, he would place it in his shoe and simply walk it out the door.

When he used the restroom during his break time, Duri Sol Ju quietly put a few pieces of chipped plastic in six different waste containers located in the hallway and in the restroom. He did this while keeping an eye open for anyone that might be in the hall observing him.

So far, so good. Now, he needed to eliminate that last pieces of the camera.

At the end of the day, Duri put the camera's processor inside his sock. Just in case someone wanted to inspect his shoes, they might miss something as thin as the processor inside his socks. He hid the tiny battery in the room, figuring it would be safer than trying to remove it. The concrete stand had flattened it, making it inoperable. He wedged it inside a metal ornament. Even if the room were scanned, it would not be spotted.

Walking up the multiple flights of steps was not as comfortable as he hoped. By the time he reached the top floor, his foot was starting to feel like he was walking with a pebble in his shoe. Actually, it was like six pieces in his shoe. The concrete stand had broken the wafer into six pieces.

Nervously, he made it past security. They didn't even look at his feet.

Leaving the building, he walked across the square and sat down to rub his foot. Even though there was snow on the ground, he took off his shoe and cautiously slipped the processor pieces out of his sock without anyone noticing.

It was a relief to get it out of there. He slipped it into his pocket and put his shoe back on.

As he headed by a trashcan, he wiped his fingerprints off the processor with a paper tissue he had saved from the restroom, wrapped it in the paper tissue, and dropped it in the can, making sure no one was watching.

Now he felt safe once again. It had been the one item that concerned him the most, since he took the picture.

That evening, one of the People's Security police was watching one of Duri Sol Ju's co-workers spending money on appliances. He was there on a tip from the worker at the store. (Store workers are often offered money to turn in anything suspicious looking in North Korea.)

They watched as he purchased a radio and a chair. In a country where money is scarce and hard goods are extremely expensive, when workers start flashing a stack of money, people pay attention.

Unknown to Duri's co-worker, the policeman reported the event to his superior.

The evening before their big adventure, Jung Chang-Sun and his friend Duri Sol Ju spoke to each other one more time before their planned escape.

They agreed that they should inform their wives that night, about the trip to the park and the barge, but not their family. If they were separated at the park, it was important that the family made it to the barge.

Jung Chang-Sun asked Duri about the chip and if he had found any information on the ship.

"It is safe. I have it in the lining of my dark coat. No one will find it unless they know where to look," he informed him. "I could not get anything more on the ship. Nevertheless, I put the name and ship number on a tiny piece of paper with the chip. It will all be there when we need it."

As they parted, they gave each other an embrace. "To freedom," Jung Chang-Sun told his friend. "May we get out of the country safely."

That evening, the police paid an unexpected visit to Duri Sol Ju's co-worker.

They took him to an interrogation area of the station and grilled him on where he had gotten the money. They didn't believe his answer that he had saved it from his salary.

The tactics of the police in North Korea are different from the rest of the world. They use intimidation, threats, and if that does not get the results they are looking for, they use violence.

After two hours of intense interrogation, he gave them a story. He told the police about how a co-worker had paid him to look at the blueprints of a building.

"What building?" the police asked.

"The Cyberwarfare Building," he answered.

"And, did you show him it?"

"Yes. He took a picture of it."

That got more than their attention.

Someone had taken a picture of the blueprints of the Cyberwarfare Building. That was top secret.

"Who was it? When did it happen?" they demanded.

He told them the whole story of how Duri Sol Ju offered to pay him to look at a blueprint. At the time, he didn't know which building he wanted to look at. When he arrived at his room, he pulled out a camera and took a picture of the blueprint. That was how he had the money.

The interrogation officer was extremely riled by the additional information.

"When?" he insisted.

"Last week."

He didn't ask any other questions. He had Duri's co-worker thrown in a holding cell until his chief officer arrived in the morning.   An immediate surveillance of Duri Sol Ju was also requested.

He wanted to know everything about him; his work, his family, where he had been.

Chapter 36

The Barge

With the celebration in the square, the morning duties at the police were that of cleaning the square and making sure everyone's uniforms were perfect for the parade. Everyone was expected to attend.

Some were monitoring the crowd while others were marching in the show of military superiority.

The North Korean leader Kim Jong-un would be there and everything had to be perfect.

The result of all the commotion for the day was that attention was not paid to the normal details. For those marching in the parade, a spot on their uniform might mean a demotion.

If anyone in the crowd misbehaved, an officer that did not react instantly might be relieved of his duty. A year ago, Kim Jong-un's vice-premier for education was executed for having improper posture during a public event. That event was still in the minds of those who attended the parade.

The result of all this attention to detail was that the police report from the evening before went unnoticed.

With all work suspended for the day, Duri Sol Ju and his family prepared for a walk to the park by the river and then to the parade route at Kim Il-sung Square.

They dressed in warm clothes. It was slightly warmer than it had been all week, but there was still a trace of snow on the ground. Winter had not yet released its final fury on North Korea. That might come at any time this late in the season.

So far, it had been an extremely warm start to winter. Some years, the bitter cold from the Arctic Circle had caused the river to freeze over by this time of the year. With high temperatures several degrees above freezing, the ice had not even started to form.

As they prepared to head to the park located by the river, Duri Sol Ju gave his wife his warm long wool jacket.

"Here, you wear it. It might be a little long, but if the kids get cold by the river, you can wrap it around you and them to stay warm. I'll wear my shorter coat."

Putting on their gloves, they headed out for the park. It was a little over a mile away from their house. To stay warm, they would stop in a restaurant for some hot tea on the way, to warm their feet before continuing on to the river.

Jung Chang-Sun and his family were about to leave as well. They had picked a different route to the park. They didn't want to appear to be traveling together with Duri Sol Ju's family.

The smaller the group, the less attention they would gather.

Neither family was excited about the parade in the Kim Il-sung Square. However, it was required and even the children were prepared to cheer the military marchers on as they had done in the past.

Jung Chang-Sun and his family had also found a restaurant to stop at and warm their feet. The hot tea was a cheap remedy to warm their bodies before continuing their walk.

Leaving the restaurant near the Kim Il-sung Square, Duri Sol Ju noticed someone that was looking at his family. It was more than a glancing look.

Something had caught the attention of this person, and for some reason, he appeared to be watching them.

They walked about a block, and when Duri looked around, the person was still behind them. He was not real close, but definitely watching them.

Duri was becoming nervous. They had come so close. Who was this man that was watching them and why? Bowibu?

He told his wife to take the kids to the park. He would take a different route and join them there – hinting that someone was watching them.

Reluctantly, she obeyed and told her husband to be careful.

Duri Sol Ju turned down a narrow street, watching to see if the man would follow.

After a few minutes, he spotted him again. He was definitely following him. *"Why?"* he thought.

Fortunately, he had only seen one man. That meant that no one was following his family.

Duri circled back around the block to the square and stopped into another restaurant.

He sat there for almost twenty minutes. He wanted to make sure no one was following him. It would give his family time to get to the park.

Now, he had to watch the time. He couldn't be late.

He went into the restroom and when he came out; he did not see any sign of the man.

Duri Sol Ju's family had made it to the park. They found an area that was blocked from the wind, and waited for Duri to join them.

So far, there was no sign of him.

They saw Jung Chang-Sun and one of his boys about fifty meters away. Another glace found his wife and his other son near a tree behind them.

They were all there. Still there was no sign of Duri.

Jung Chang-Sun became concerned when he saw Duri's wife and sons without Duri. He wondered what had happened. Why wasn't he in the park?

After a few minutes, he told his son to go over by his mother and he walked over to where Duri's wife was standing.

"It is a lovely day for a walk, where is Duri?" he asked.

Duri's wife answered, "He thought someone was watching him. He left us and told me he would join us shortly.

I am getting worried. I have not seen him since."

It was a dilemma for all of them. Had Duri Sol Ju slipped up and someone found out about their plans? Perhaps, he was just overly cautious and would appear at the last minute to catch the barge.

Jung Chang-Sun noticed that Duri's wife was wearing Duri's long winter coat. Had he had a premonition of the events of the day?

It was hard for Jung Chang-Sun to convince Duri's wife that she should not be concerned. If something did happen, they might all be arrested and thrown in prison.

Chapter 37

Mistakes

Time was running out and Duri Sol Ju needed to get to the park.

After looking for the person that was following him, Duri tried to use a back door to the restaurant to elude whomever the person was that had been watching him, just in case he was still out there.

As he left the building, he was stopped by the police.

"Why are you stopping me?" he asked. "I have done nothing wrong."

"We had a report of a man wearing the same coat yesterday that stole food from the market. The man over there identified you as the man."

"But, I was not at the market yesterday. I work at the Grand People's Study House all day. I clean the antiquities.

"Besides, I wear my long wool coat to work every day. You could ask the security people. They know me."

"Perhaps, but you will have to go with us. The doors are locked at the Grand People's Study House right now, because of the parade in the square. We can check out your story tomorrow when it opens."

Duri Sol Ju's heart sank. He knew there was no sense resisting. If he did, they might go looking for his family. Then, everyone would be in danger.

He had no choice; he had to let them take him to wherever they were going. He wished he had a way of letting his family know what had happened.

The police officer led him away and put him in a holding cell until morning.

At the park, everyone was extremely worried. What had happened to Duri? Was he going to appear at the last minute, or would they have to leave without him.

The contact was emphatic. The barge would not wait. If Duri was late, they would leave without him.

Jung Chang-Sun's wife was wondering what he was doing over with Duri's wife. Where was Duri?

She had orders not to leave the tree they were standing by until someone from the barge made contact with them. Now, she stood there wondering what was happening.

Had something gone wrong? Would the barge still come?

A few minutes before noon, a barge appeared upriver. It was not very big. It was a river barge designed for hauling supplies up and down shallow rivers. It was probably fifty meters long.

Even though it was still up river, they could hear the diesel engine chugging along as it slowly approached.

Duri's wife was still looking around hoping to see Duri appear in the park.

"Don't look," Jung Chang-Sun told her. Someone might see you watching for someone and become suspicious.

"He'll find a way to get here."

She understood the suggestion. She realized she had to be concerned for her sons even if Duri missed the boat.

The barge pulled up to the small dock, and Jung Chang-Sun saw his contact jump off to tie it off to the dock. He gave a short wave for them to come to the barge.

"Go," he told Duri's wife. Then, he motioned to his wife to get on the barge.

"As Duri's wife moved towards the barge, her son asked her why they were going to the boat?"

"Just get onboard. Keep quiet," she instructed them.

"But, where is Papa," he asked.

"He'll come," she answered. "Now, get onboard."

They climbed aboard the barge and slipped into the cargo area. As they did, Duri's wife took one more look to see if she could see Duri coming out of the shadows.

There was no sign of him.

The barge operators were keeping an eye open for people paying too much attention to their stop as well. It was a risk for them to stop this close to the square.

As Jung Chang-Sun's family got aboard, his contact asked him, "Where is your friend?"

"He was worried he was followed and took another route. Can you give him a few minutes?"

"No, I have my orders. The longer we sit, the more danger we are in. We must leave," he insisted. "Where is the information?"

"We have it," Jung Chang-Sun answered. "I'll give it to you when we are safe."

They took one more look in the park for Duri. He was not there.

The captain told them, "Time to leave."

Reluctantly, they untied the lines and pulled away from the dock.

The captain told them he would keep watch as they passed down river. If he saw anyone trying to wave them over, he would let them see if it was Duri Sol Ju.

The group was hidden behind some empty crates in the bottom of the barge. With the slow boat, they would be there for a while. Fortunately, their contact had brought food and water for the family.

Unfortunately, it was almost dark down there. There was only one small light by the ladder leading to the hatch.

"Get some rest," their contact told them. "It is going to be a long day."

It was not very warm in the bottom of the barge. The water temperature determined the barge's temperature. Fortunately, it was not much colder than their homes this time of the year.

Jung Chang-Sun looked over at Duri's wife. He could see a tear in her eyes. It would be hard to explain to her sons that they might never see their father again.

It appeared that Jung Chang-Sun's contact had been correct. Everyone was heading to the square and not paying attention to a lone barge heading down river. There were lines of people headed toward the Kim Il-sung Square in the center of town.

As the boat rounded the large island in the middle of the river, even the military academy was void of people. They had all headed for the square or already standing in line for the start of the military parade. It was a good sign.

It was a quiet trip down river to the ocean. With the drone of the diesel engine the boys fell asleep quickly, all snuggled together behind the crate.

"How long will it take?" Duri Sol Ju's wife asked me.

"I'm not sure. At the speed the barge was coming down river, it might take overnight. I'm sure when we are in a safe area; they will come talk to us."

I really wanted to give her a reassuring hug to let her know it would be okay. I couldn't imagine what was going through her mind. My mind was already racing. What was she thinking about?

We still couldn't talk about what we did. If something happened, it was best that the boys knew nothing about it.

About four hours later, I heard the sound of a boat close by. I motioned to the others to be silent. We didn't want to let anyone know we were in the barge.

The boat came along side. I could hear the captain talking to someone. It sounded like a patrol boat. He was telling them that he was on his regular trip across the Yellow Sea to Dalian, China.

With the patrol boat, I figured we had reached the harbor at Nampo. There were patrols there that prevented ships from exiting or entering the harbor without the Navy's okay.

Soon, we were underway once again. They never did search the cargo area. Perhaps this was the person our contact had hinted about when he said he had things under control. It was while we were at sea that he was concerned.

Once we were at sea, the barge had a definite roll. We were pleased that it was not bad weather.

Our contact opened the hatch and came down to talk to us. It was a welcome sight.

"I'm sorry; we kept a field glass on the shoreline. We didn't see anyone trying to flag us down. I'm afraid your friend will be on his own."

It was not what Duri's wife wanted to hear. However, she was pleased to hear that they had been watching for him since she could not go up on deck and watch for Duri herself.

He explained that it could take twenty-four hours to reach the China mainland. He would leave the hatch partially open so we could get fresh air. However, they would shut it if it started to get rough.

For safety, they did not want water to enter the barge.

"If you need to use the restroom, or want a short visit topside, you could come up a couple at a time to the pilot house.

The crew will be watching for other ships. If there were any ships nearby, we would ask you to stay below. They have better glasses than we do. We don't want them to see we have passengers," he informed us.

"It's going to be a long trip. When you are not sleeping, take the invitation to come topside. The fresh air and movement will do you good. Besides, the boys may want to see how a boat crosses an ocean. They can watch the radar.

We are watching the radar constantly to make sure a North Korean military boat doesn't sneak up on us when we aren't looking.

He turned to Jung Chang-Sun. "You have the information on you?" he asked once again.

Jung Chang –Sun answered, "Yes. As I told you before, I will give it to you once we are safely in China."

"Very good. Can you tell me if you found the location of both buildings?"

"Yes. I could see why they were hard to find. I have the location of both and the picture of the blueprint of the Cyberwarfare Building."

With that information, our contact headed back to the pilothouse. The fresh air coming in the cracked hatch made it more comfortable down below. The warm currents of the Yellow Sea actually made it warmer in the barge.

We all wondered what happed to Duri. Was he safe? Did the military pick him up? We would probably never know.

Chapter 38

Change in Plans

We made several trips topside at night for restroom trips and to stretch. It was peaceful at night. There were no signs of other ships, and the stars were shining brightly.

The captain showed the boys how they navigated at night. Every once in a while a ship would appear on the long-range radar. The captain would watch to see if they changed course to one that might intercept our planned route.

So far, no one was paying attention to a small slow barge crossing the Yellow Sea.

Washington DC.

CIA headquarters received a message that Operation Blue had a glitch. Top-level agents quickly gathered to assess the situation.

Word had come from an agent in North Korea that Duri Sol Ju was picked up by the People's Security police. He had been arrested for stealing from the market. So far, he was being held in a holding cell in Pyongyang.

The good news was that the rest of the group was on the barge and it had cleared the North Korean harbor at Nampo.

That put it out to sea.

"Do they know anything about Duri Sol Ju at the police station other than they think he stole something at the market?" an agent asked.

"As far as we can tell, no. However, if they smell any nervousness with his interrogation, who knows what he may be forced to tell them."

"Did he take something from the market?" another agent asked.

"Who cares. In North Korea, they can put you away for life for saying a single word against their Supreme Chairman. They might make an example out of him for stealing a melon.

"I think we may have a problem."

They sat and discussed their options.

The barge would take at least another twenty-two hours to reach Chinese waters. Until that point, North Korea could intercept the barge if they had any hint the families were onboard.

The CIA decided, if the families had indeed obtained the information they needed, it would be lost if the barge was intercepted.

They decided to talk to their Chinese contacts, to see if they could offer any options.

<u>Yellow Sea</u>

It was two in the morning when someone came down the ladder into the barge. It was our contact.

"Jung Chang-Sun, I just got a call on my satellite phone. We have a change in plans. They want us to change course and head slightly south. I just want to let you know, so that you do not get worried if you see that we were not heading straight west," he informed us.

"Are we heading for South Korea? I asked.

"No, they would be watching for any boats that turned towards the South Korean coast. We are heading for open waters.

"It will be safer. The North Korean patrol boats do not like to travel that far from their waters."

It sounded like a good explanation. I just wondered why they changed the route at this late point in time.

Around 4:00 am, we heard the engines slow. It was not a good sign. The hatch had not been shut.

Was there a boat in the area? I worried that this might be a drop off point for our trip. They might try to force us to give up our information and then throw us into the sea. It would be safer for the crew.

I was glad I had not given them the information earlier. So far, there was a chance that I was the only one onboard that knew where the information was hidden.

About fifteen minutes later, our contact came down to talk to us.

"It is still dark outside. We have been instructed to go slow in this area. They are going to send a boat to meet us. It will get you to safety quicker.

"When it arrives, there is a slight chop to the waters. You will need to be careful with the boys, and hold their hands tightly. You don't want them to slip into the water."

"Will you be coming also," I asked.

"No. I am on the ship's manifest. If I do not show up with the ship, I will be listed as missing at sea. That could be a problem and people would be looking into my background. I need to show up at the port.

"Don't worry; you will be taken care of. You might even get a warm meal. I'll let you know when we spot the boat."

A boat? I was hoping for a fast ship. Now, I was expecting to see some smugglers boat with a large motor on it. That didn't sound any safer.

About 4:45 am, we heard the engines stop. It was a puzzling quiet.

We hadn't heard the sound of the engines of another boat through the hull. We sat there silently worrying what was going on.

Fortunately, the boys were still sleeping.

Duri's wife turned to me. "Jung, what is happening?" she asked.

"I do not know. I did not hear a boat. I do not like the feeling I have."

I hated the words I just said. I should have been convincing that everything was okay. The problem was, I wasn't sure either.

From the hatch, I heard the words of our contact person. "Please come quickly. The boat has arrived and you need to leave."

It did not have the sound the way I was hoping. I mentioned to the others to let me lead the way to see if it was safe. They could follow when I was sure we were not heading for a quick swim.

Actually, at that point, we probably didn't have any options. We were at the mercy of the crew.

As I peered out of the hatch, I was surprised. There were two rubber boats paddling towards us. They were only five meters from our barge. Where had they come from? In the dark, I could hardly see my own hands. Now, even the pilothouse lights were off. The only light came from the partial moon up in the sky.

From the dim light of the red light lite under the hatchway by the ladder leading up, I motioned for the others to join me.

From their silence, I could tell everyone was afraid.

Poking my head back topside once again, I asked, "Where is the boat?"

Our contact person pointed, "Out there."

It was dark. It took my eyes a minute to adjust to how dark it was even though we had only the single light inside the barge.

As I looked carefully, I could just make out the shape of a long boat sitting low to the water about thirty meters from our barge. If it wasn't for the slight reflection of the waves washing over the deck, I might have missed it.

There it was. Someone had sent a submarine to pick us up. Were we that important? Obviously, someone wanted the information very badly.

256

Quickly, we grabbed everyone's hands and we got up on the edge of the deck of the barge.

The crew split us up. One family in one rubber raft, the rest in the other raft.

I heard our contact shout, "Good luck." With that, our new crew started to swiftly paddle us to our new boat.

They were very skilled at what they were doing. It only took a few minutes for four seamen in each boat to paddle us to the submarine.

In less than ten minutes, we were inside the boat, and the crew and their equipment were safely tucked inside as well.

"Welcome to the USS Cheyenne," a person greeted us in what sounded like a South Korean dialect. "I am Ensign Ritter. Please follow me. We need to dive quickly below the surface. When we level off, out of sight, the Captain and I will greet you properly. We are not sure the North Korean Navy would like to know that we are out here," he told us.

We followed him to the food service area they called the mess, and sat at some booths. As we sat there, we could feel the ships nose gently dip as we dropped below the surface.

So, this was why I had not heard another boat in the water earlier. The submarine was totally silent. There was no motor sound. Even though it was twice as long as the barge we had been on, in the darkness of the night, I hardly realized it was floating a stone's throw from the barge.

Everyone sat wondering what we were about to experience. For the boys, they were worried the boat would sink. I tried to explain to them that it was designed to stay underwater for weeks at a time. It would be safe.

Our Korean-speaking officer told the boys that they were safe. Asking how long it had been since we had a hot meal, he asked the boys if they would like some eggs and pancakes. For them pancakes was a new term. Soon, they would learn to like the hospitality of the submarine.

The Captain joined us about thirty minutes later. With his interpreter, Ensign Ritter, he explained to us that their Chinese contacts had informed them that Duri Sol Ju had been picked up for stealing something at a market.

"That's not so," his wife stated.

"I'm sure you are right," he said. "Unfortunately, the North Korean police are hard to convince.

"We were worried that they might force him to say where you were. They might send a fast patrol boat out looking for the slow barge. The decision was made to pick you up and to get you to safety.

"I'm told you have some information for us," the interpreter said as the Captain looked directly at me.

I didn't know what to do at that point, so I pointed at Duri's wife's coat. "It is in there," I told him.

One of the crewmen brought it over to me.

I showed them where it was sewn under the lining.

Another member of the crew brought a sharp surgical knife over and opened the seam. There, under the liner was the small camera chip, and a small piece of soft silk paper with a set of numbers on it. It was the location of the buildings they had asked for.

The translator asked, "What is this other number?"

I told him it was the location of Room 39. "It was in a ship in the harbor. That's why we could not find the blueprint. It was not a building, it was a supply ship."

The Captain motioned to a crewmember to take the chip along with the information and transmit it ASAP, when they could send a signal.

Then, they both sat down and explained to us the little information they had about our future.

They were taking us to a harbor in Japan. It would take the boat until the middle of the next night to get there.

We were shown the quarters where we could lay down and sleep. It was an area we could be in while we were underway. He asked that we stay in this area unless we had permission to move about.

Our translator, Ensign Ritter, would stay close to us if we needed anything.

Once we were in friendly water, if the boys would like a tour of parts of the boat, we can show them how we steer a submarine.

With that, he left to command the submarine.

Chapter 39

Information

Washington DC.

CIA headquarters was ecstatic to receive the information that was transmitted from the submarine. While the sun hadn't risen yet over the Yellow Sea, the wheels were already spinning at the Pentagon.

News that mysterious Room 39 was located and that it was on a supply ship in the harbor surprised even the best surveillance officers at the CIA.

If they had known that, they could have taken North Korea's five million dollar (U.S.) printing press out of service a long time ago.

Now, the concern was shifted to what happened to Duri Sol Ju. If Duri Sol Ju talked about taking photos, he might mention Room 39. If the North Koreans knew the U.S. was aware of the location of the press, they could quickly dismantle it and move it to another location. It might take years to locate it again.

The other piece of information that surprised them was the location of the Cyberwarfare Building.

According to the information from the submarine, they had indicated that it was located directly below the Kim Il-sung Square.

According to the blueprints, there were tunnels that led from several locations including the Grand People's Study House.

That was how they got their teams of computer experts in and out without people noticing a large number of computer nerds at any one location. It was brilliant. Who would have looked under the square?

The information was relayed to the White House for the morning briefing session.

Now, it was up to the generals and the President as to what they wanted to do with the information.

Pyongyang North Korea

The Chief Political Officer at the police station was irate when he saw the note the officer had left for him after interrogating Duri Sol Ju's co-worker.

"Why was I not shown this yesterday?" he demanded from his officers.

"Everyone was at the square. It was by orders of our Supreme Chairman Kim Jung-un. What were we to do? It was his orders," one of the officers answered.

As he read the full report, he shouted, "Where is this man – Duri Sol Ju. I want him found immediately. Now! Understand?"

Immediately, people were scattering asking officers to begin a citywide search.

About fifteen minutes later, an officer came back in. "He is here – in our holding area. He has been here since yesterday morning. He was arrested because he had a jacket on similar to someone who stole something at the market.

"We checked with the security people where he works at the Grand People's Study Hall, at a secure level. They said he was there all day the day before and had worn a different coat. He was not the man that was in the market.

"We were about to release him."

The Chief Officer's face turned redder. "Do not release that man. I want him put in irons and interrogated immediately.

"I have a letter from two nights ago, saying he copied blueprints for secret buildings in the city. I want to know where that information went to and who he was working with. Now! Do you understand?"

Once again, police officers were on the move. This case had just been put on the highest priority. The Chief Officer knew that once information about the espionage reached Kim Jung-un, if they did not have answers, at best, he would lose his job. At worst???

He contacted the Commander of the Bowibu and told him about the report. The Commander was furious when he heard the news.

Duri Sol Ju held out for five grueling hours. Because of the severity of the offense that his co-worker had admitted being a part of, his interrogators held back nothing attempting to quickly get a confession out of Duri. They wanted the information about his accomplices.

By mid-afternoon, Duri Sol Ju's face looked like something hanging in a meat market. His back and sides were not much better. Finally, after nearly drowning him, he broke.

Duri Sol Ju told them of the plan. He and his friend Jung Chang-Sun had planned to remove a drawing from the secret room and sell it on the black market in China.

He told them how a contact had asked them to take a picture of the blueprints of two buildings. They gave him a camera to use. After he talked his co-worker into letting him take the picture, he destroyed the camera.

"Where is the picture now?" they insisted.

Reluctantly, he told them, "We were to take a barge to China. It is on the barge. I was on the way to the barge when I was arrested."

His interrogators immediately left the room. An immediate set of phone calls found one barge was seen heading down-river at the time of Duri Sol Ju's arrest.

Now, they knew the name of the boat, and where it was heading.

The North Korean air force scrambled two of their jets. Their mission, sink the barge before it makes Chinese waters.

The barge was within miles of official Chinese waters when the jets picked it up on radar. They were so intent on their target that they missed three Chinese jets heading their way.

By the time the radar in the North Korean jets picked up the Chinese jets, it was too late. There were four heat-seeking missiles headed towards the North Korean jets.

As they attempted to elude the missiles, one of the North Korean jets managed to get one air to surface missiles off from his jet.

Seconds later, the Chinese planes missiles scored direct hits on the North Korean jets. The fell into the water as burning chunks of metal.

There were no signs that the crew made it out.

Unfortunately, a minute later, there was an explosion on the sea. The single missile had managed to lock into the slow moving barge and made a direct hit on the cargo compartment.

As the jets circled the barge, they spotted the crew launching a lifeboat. Somehow, they manage to escape the blast.

The jets radioed the information to the Chinese Navy, who sent a cruiser out to rescue the crew of the barge.

The North Korean military picked up on the Chinese radio communications. For North Korea, it was another embarrassment.

The incident never made the news.

Washington DC.

CIA headquarters was monitoring all the movements of Operation Blue. Word of the attack on the barge and the downing of the North Korean jets spread quickly within the agency.

After a brief meeting, it was decided that they needed to move up their plans for the completion of Operation Blue. The sinking of the barge was an indication that the North Koreans had broken Duri Sol Ju. It was determined that he had probably given them the information they required about his espionage.

Now, before North Korea had a chance to make any changes, the White House gave the go-ahead to start phase two of Operation Blue.

It would begin immediately.

Chapter 40

Delayed Plans

USS Cheyenne – Yellow Sea

The USS Cheyenne had traveled only about an hour from the pickup point of the North Koreans. The group was starting to become acquainted with traveling underwater.

The boat was just exiting the unofficial extension of North Korean waters claimed by both China and North Korea, and was officially in international water.

As the Captain of the boat was starting to relax after setting his course and making sure the boat was secured, his break was interrupted by his message center.

"Captain, this is Lieutenant Commander Short. The ship's sonar expert has picked up the sound of an explosion in the water. He had projected it to be in the general area where the North Korean barge would have been heading, if it stayed on course. In addition, he also reported the sound of debris hitting the water."

It was what Washington had expected. Somehow, the North Koreans had figured out the exit plan and must have met up with the barge. If the families had not been extricated from the barge, all the information would have probably been lost, and Operation Blue would have come to an abrupt end.

The Captain replied back, "Thank you. Keep me informed if we get any additional messages, or if you pick up any traffic in our area."

The submarine was one of the quietest in the fleet. It had been designed to run silent and deep. With its advanced sonar and computer systems, it could detect an explosion over a hundred miles away when it was underway and deep under the water.

Unless the submarine made a mistake, the North Korean's would never know they were in the area. Even the Russians could not keep track of the U.S. submarines when they went dark in the water.

It was only an hour later that the Captain was interrupted once again. This time it was the radio operator.

"Captain, we have a message coming in."

"What is it?" the Captain asked.

"Urgent Flash traffic. They want to talk to us."

"Okay, take us up to periscopes depth. Let's see what is so urgent."

The Captain headed up to the helm.

"What's the surface conditions?" he asked.

"Sun is rising and it is fully overcast with a light chop. No traffic so far. We should be hard to spot," was the answer given by his Lieutenant Commander.

"Very good, raise the antenna. Let's see what's so important."

It only took a few minutes for the communications between the submarine and Naval Operations, PACOM, to transmit the new orders, and for the boat to acknowledge what they were expected to do.

When the transmissions were over, the antenna was lowered. Once again, the boat slipped back, diving deeper in the water. Only, this time, it was turning to a new course.

The Captain turned to Lieutenant Commander Short. "Notify the Seal Team Commander, I want a meeting with him in fifteen minutes. We have a change in plans. We are heading back."

There was always a small Seal Team aboard the submarine. They were trained for all kinds of operations.

As the Captain sat down with the Commander of the team, he showed him the confidential orders that had just come in.

"They want us to return to North Korea," he told him. "I'm not sure what is so special, but we have orders to sink a boat in the harbor at Nampo." He handed him a copy of the orders.

The Captain told them, "They have transmitted a harbor map showing the location of the ship. Apparently, it is a supply ship, which is sitting at the docks.

"The message said to have the Seal Team sink it discreetly. I assume that means they want you to swim in and plant explosives.

"We can get you close to the harbor. The water depth is good and provided we do not detect fishing nets or boats, we can get you within a couple miles. I'll have navigation pull the harbor maps for you.

"I'll let you and your men have time to prepare your gear to get you in there, and as soon as I have an arrival time plotted, I'll let you know."

The Commander thanked the Captain. Then, he left immediately, and went below to meet with his team.

After the Captain's meeting, he met with Ensign Ritter and explained the new situation. It would be up to Ensign Ritter to explain to his party that we were asked to delay their delivery.

He would also need to explain that for the next six to eight hours, the boat would be running silently. All talking would be held to a minimum and nothing dropped.

Ensign Ritter acknowledged the request. He would stay with the families and make sure they were silent. He suggested having them eat something now so that they could be resting when the submarine reached its destination.

Ensign Ritter went below, and met with the families.

"The Captain has requested that I meet with you and explain that we have a slight delay in getting you to shore.

"We have been requested to gather some information before we return. Because of this, we will be in shallow water and do not want anyone to detect our presence. It means that we will have to be sitting dead quiet on the bottom for a few hours.

"I suggested that we give you a chance to eat before we get there. We will only have about an hour before we go quiet. After that, if you can stay quiet in your area, it will be best for all of us."

Jung Chang-Sun and Duri Sol Ju's wife understood. Whatever the Captain ordered, that's what they would do. Quickly, they got the kids up and as a group, they moved to the mess area.

While they were eating, or should we say, picking at their new foods, the parents emphasized to the children that it would be important to sit or lay quietly for a while, at least until they were told they could move around.

At this point, they were so petrified of the whole adventure; they were willing to do anything their parents told them.

Washington DC.

Operation Blue was rolling out. With the location of the Cyberwarfare Building, it made penetration very difficult.

A bunker-busting bomb might take it out. However, dropping one on a nation without declaring war would result in a full war with North Korea and perhaps even with Russia. It would also risk North Korea launching one of their nuclear missiles.

A second concept had been worked out after locating the building. Intelligence gathered over the years had located the power grid for the city. They knew where the main feeders were located for each area of the city.

A complex such as this probably had backup generators. However, since it was underground, the generators needed to be above ground or at least have exhaust above ground.

On top of that, they had to have a massive set of routers for their computers to tie into the internet. Without that equipment, they could not disrupt companies and hold them for ransomware.

By knowing the location of the building, U.S. intelligence could locate the switching routers used in the Pyongyang cyberwarfare operation and determine how they connected to the internet.

The concept was developed a few years ago and tested on a small scale in the U.S. to see if it would work.

An electronic bug would be sent to the power sub-station that supplied that area of Pyongyang. It would temporarily show an overload and the system, which would automatically shut down the electrical system to prevent problems.

Within a few minutes, engineers would probably reset the system and restart the flow of power to the area.

In the meanwhile, the backup generators would kick in to supply power to the computer area and routers. There would be a short delay as the routers came back on line.

It was during that delay, and reconnection with the internet, that software engineers planned to send a malware packet to the routers. Detection software in North Korea would be inactive for that few seconds the reconnection occurred. Once the packet was on the server, it could reproduce itself to all the computers and systems connected to it.

At a set time, it would start a worm that would infect all of their systems. Even with good backups, it would take weeks before they reestablished their operation.

With luck, if they did not remove the entire worm, their backups would become infected as well. It might put them out of business for a very long time.

The White House gave the go ahead for the next phase of Operation Blue.

Over the next twenty-four hours, the worm would start to penetrate North Korea's system.

Chapter 41

Deployment

USS Cheyenne – Yellow Sea

The USS Cheyenne had retraced its tracks back to the harbor of Nampo. They were sitting ten miles off shore, hugging close to the bottom at a good water depth.

The boat had been rigged for silent operations, and the Seal Team had their gear ready to penetrate the North Korean harbor.

Compared to other operations, this was the most sensitive deployment this team had been involved with. Detection was not an option. They needed to get in and out quickly and silently. Then, only after the submarine was out in international waters, the targeted ship would be sunk.

If anything went wrong, it could start a war the U.S. and their allies did not want to see.

As all systems were checked and readied for the underwater entrance to the harbor, the Captain gave the order to proceed at dead slow, and head closer to shore. They would move to a point two miles off shore and slightly to the south of the harbor entrance.

Ensign Ritter stayed with the families in their area to make sure everything was under control. They were asked to stay in their bunks until he changed the orders.

Once on location, the Seal Team silently slipped out of the airlocks and deployed their underwater propulsion unit as the submarine gently sat on the bottom.

Now, for the men and women on the submarine, it was simply a waiting game. The submarine slipped back into the safer, deeper water, settling to the bottom. There it watched for all surface traffic that might head their way.

The Seal Team moved out from the submarine, to the entrance of the harbor.

When a slow moving barge was spotted coming in from the Yellow Sea, to head up river, they stayed close to the wake of the barge, preventing any underwater noise detection systems in the harbor from picking them up.

It only took about an hour to reach their destination. They detached and left their propulsion unit on the bottom of the river. Just in case there were any active sound detection systems on the ship, it was quieter and less detectable to leave their propulsion system out in the river. From there it was a short swim over to the ship.

Reaching the supply ship, magnetic detonators were placed strategically along the one side of the hull. Once they were set off, they would sink the ship, and if all went to plan, cause it to roll away from the pier.

That would prevent anyone from unloading its cargo if the vessel did not successfully sink to the bottom.

It didn't take long to finish the task.

With the assistance of the Taedong River's current, it only took an additional forty-five minutes to return to the predetermined location where the submarine was expecting to meet them.

When they arrived at the designated location, the submarine was just settling to the bottom.

The crew quickly opened the hatch to the air locks, slipped inside and stored their equipment.

Less than twenty minutes after the Seal Team had opened the air locks, with the Seal Team safely onboard, the USS Cheyenne lifted off the bottom. Then, it silently slipped back out of North Korean waters. Soon, the submarine would be in international waters.

For anyone in the harbor, there had been nothing to indicate there had been any visitors.

It was thirty minutes later that the sonar operator reported to the Captain that multiple explosions were picked up coming from the harbor. The timed detonators had gone off.

Once in international waters, the ship proceeded back on its original course for a Japanese port to off-load their passengers.

Washington DC.

From an agent in North Korea, the CIA received the report on the sinking of a supply ship in the Nampo harbor.

The agent reported that he had spotted the ship listing over before sinking to the bottom. From his report, it sounded as if the operation had been a success.

The hull of the ship was deep enough in the water that any cargo would have been damaged by the brackish waters of the harbor.

To the Operations Managers in Washington, it was a complete success. The five million dollar intaglio printing press would be unusable by the time they raised the ship off the bottom of the harbor. Washington's only hope was that the ship was loaded with printed money that had not been off-loaded in the past day. If that were the case, it would have been the icing on the cake.

The operation had been completed as planned. There had been no evidence that a U.S. Seal Team had penetrated North Korean waters. To the world, the ship simply had an explosion and sunk.

The only people in North Korea that knew something was amiss was the recovery team that had to move the ship from the pier. Twisted pieces of hull pointing inward would indicate the explosion came from the outside of the hull.

Whether that information would be given to Kim Jung-un was unknown. If it were disclosed that someone had penetrated the harbor without detection, firing squads would have some target practice once again.

A message was transmitted to the USS Cheyenne from Naval Operations (PACOM).

It simply said, "Job well done. Ship listing on harbor bottom."

Aboard the USS Cheyenne, the Captain congratulated the Seal Team, and rigged for normal running under nuclear power. Away from the harbor, noises onboard the boat would not be picked up by ships in the area.

Then, he sent a transmission to Naval Operations (PATCOM) that included his estimated arrival time.

Pyongyang North Korea

It had not been a very good day for the North Korean military establishment. Besides losing three interceptor jets, they realized that the espionage by Duri Sol Ju had cost them an operation worth billions of Won to their economy, per year. It might take years to re-establish their printing industry.

Their follow-up investigation after Duri Sol Ju's confession put them on the track of Jung Chang-Sun. When they searched the homes of the two families, it was as if they simply went for a walk and never returned. Nothing was packed. Everything was still as they left it.

It was assumed from the tale Duri Sol Ju had told his interrogators, both families were on the barge that was sunk in the Yellow Sea.

Reports of a few crewmembers being rescued by a Chinese ship did not indicate that any other people had survived. Observers on shore when the crew was brought in for medical treatment did not indicate any additional survivors.

The North Korean government assumed everyone was in the cargo area and went down with the barge.

With an already struggling economy, they would not be able to replace the loss in currency. Cutbacks would be needed, and it was coming at a critical time. The military had put all their resources into missile development. A worldwide challenge had been given by their leader that North Korea was to be a country that needed to be respected.

A special cabinet meeting was setup for the following day to discuss financial options.

Knowing their leader's temper, it was a meeting that no one wanted to attend.

The following day, at the high-level cabinet meeting, Supreme Chairman Kim Jung-un was livid. He insisted on immediate demotions for those responsible for their inability to prevent such actions.

As a result, the Chief Officer of the People's Security police in Pyongyang was executed for his inability to perform his job.

When Kim Jung-un learned that the country's printing of foreign currency had slowed in the past months due to reallocation of funds to the missile program, his anger grew.

He hoped that they had a warehouse full of currency they could drop on the market to sustain the country during the winter months.

Supreme Chairman Kim Jung-un put additional pressure on his finance minister. "Find sources of money immediately."

He knew that Russia and China were reluctant to issue any additional loans. The country had burned too many bridges in the past couple years to depend on their assistance.

Unfortunately, the immediate solution was to cut expenses. That would mean cutting outside food purchases and probably reducing the military's food and clothing allowances. There had to be sacrifices and this one was dipping all the way down to the military.

As the meeting was breaking up, there was a flicker in the lights. Then, the power went off for a minute until the backup generators kicked in.

Kim Jung-un shook his head. "We can't even depend on our power today. Find out what's going on and fix it," he shouted.

Then, he stormed out of the room.

Chapter 42

Mopping Up

<u>Hong Kong</u>

The Chinese government wasted little time in shutting down the Chen-Lee Tea Company and the remainder of their organization once Operation Blue was completed. The smugglers knew they had limited time remaining before their freedom would end.

The owner of the company was expected to receive a five-year sentence after assisting in the subsequent operation. His black market associates would also find prison time.

The Chinese government was pleased to eliminate one of the major routes for the selling and removal of antiquities held by North Korea. Now, the struggle would be an attempt to retrieve any treasures that they could find.

For their cooperation, the U.S. government agreed to return many of the confiscated items that they had seized in the past few years, which the "organization" had brought to the U.S., and had historically originated in China.

The rest of the confiscated items would remain in sealed containers in a warehouse, somewhere, until a country could provide the proper paper claim to their items.

__USS Cheyenne__

It took until the next day before the USS Cheyenne reached Japanese waters.

The USS Cheyenne finally made port at the U.S. base in Okinawa, Japan. Under the cover of night, she off-loaded her passengers.

There was never any word released of her assignment.

Once the passengers were off, the ship was resupplied, and silently sailed off to continue her assignment.

It had been a very successful deployment and the morale of the crew was high after the cruise.

The Seal Team received commendations for their work.

Now, the families that had endured their escape from North Korea and were onboard the USS Cheyenne, were whisked away to a location on the base for interrogation prior to reassignment to an unknown location.

Even though the information they provided had been extremely helpful, the CIA wanted to make sure that they were not counteragents for the North Korean military.

Their stay at the base would only be for a few weeks before being brought to another location for additional transitioning.

Washington DC.

At the next morning briefing, the President was brought up to speed on success of Operation Blue.

The sinking of the ship containing Room 39 appeared to be a complete success. According to sources in North Korea, there had been no evidence that the North Koreans had removed anything from the ship prior to its sinking in the harbor.

If the press used for making foreign currency had been in the ship, it would have been destroyed by the corrosion caused by the brackish salt water of the harbor.

If the operation had been delayed by even one day, the outcome might have been different.

In a second report from the U.S. Counterintelligence Agency, it was reported, "The signals received from the internet nodes in North Korea indicated that the malware worm had been deployed into the routers and computers of the North Korean Cyberwarfare Building.

"Computer traffic coming from that location to the internet node appeared to have stopped. All the indications we have are suggesting that the worm had worked by infecting North Korea's system used for creating ransomware throughout the world.

"We are still determining the full extent of the operation, and estimate that it will take some time to determine if North Korea had adequate backup systems in place to prevent the worm from destroying any immediate attempts to reinstate their software."

Everyone at the meeting had a slight smile on their face.

There was one side concern of the operation. It was the concern that other countries might determine how the U.S.

disabled the North Korean operation, and create similar bugs that could be used in other locations.

The President thanked his military advisors for the information and told his heads of staff, "Now, we wait and see. Without funding, how long will North Korea's Kim Jung-un be able to stay in power?

"If he falls in disgrace with the military, the question is; who will replace him.

"Let's run some possibilities just in case. Also, run some options on programs we can offer them if they are willing to change their leadership.

"If we are lucky, we might get the people of North Korea to end the current threats of war and dismantle their nuclear programs."

Chapter 43

Settlement

Three Months Later – Minneapolis, Minnesota

A plane landed at the Minneapolis International Airport. On board were seven North Korean refugees. It had been a long flight and they were very tired.

Customs Agent Olson, a Korean interpreter, and a representative from the FBI – Agent Alex North, met the plane's passengers at the security area.

They were there at the request of Washington to assist the group getting through the complications of U.S. Customs.

They had been told that the refugees were part of a resettlement program promised by the CIA for their cooperation in North Korea. Other than that information, all the information the group had was the work and location background supplied by the resettlement camp they had been at for the past three months.

During that time, they learned some basic English and bits and pieces of American culture. It was hoped that it would ease the strains of moving to a new country.

The program set out by the State Department, was to establish the families in a location in Minnesota where there was a South Korean heritage. Since the languages were very similar, although cultures were strained over the past fifty years, it was hoped that it would ease the transition to American life here in the States.

For their protection, their names would be changed. They would be given Americanized names to prevent any possible future threats from North Korea.

It was unlikely that North Korean agents would hunt for them; however, it was a safety precaution just in case.

Customs Agent Olson explained to the group, through an interpreter, that his job was to make sure they got through Customs without problems. At this point, he would turn them and the interpreter over to FBI Agent Alex North, who would be there to assist them in making a safe resettlement.

Going out of her way because of the exhausted looking families, Alex helped them gather their luggage and drove them to a townhouse located just outside of Minneapolis. There, she helped them move into their new homes. It was a good location. It had been picked because there were several Korean families in the complex.

She made sure that the families were familiar with the appliances in the homes. Many of the appliances did not exist in North Korea.

She assumed the relocation center had taught them the basics, but she knew that it was important for the families to feel comfortable as quickly as possible in their new settings.

Alex also showed them where a charter school was nearby. It would help them learn English and attempt to teach the children the basics they might have missed in North Korean schools.

It was important that they start to catch up to the other students as quickly as possible. The goal was to have them mainstreamed within a year.

There were daytime and evening classes for adults at the school as well.

She also told them that they would have a social worker assigned to them, to assist in many things including transportation, medical needs and other things that might come up. Apparently, they were told that already and knew that the government would provide them with funding for a few years to assist them while they secured a job and assimilated into society.

For now, it was Alex's job to protect them and make sure their transition went smoothly. It was something new to her as well. This was the first resettlement she had handled. The State Department wanted to make sure there were no threats to the family due to their North Korean heritage.

With the help of an interpreter, after making sure they had a refrigerator full of food, she sat and talked with them for a while, making enough contact that the families would trust her enough to call if they had a problem. It was an interesting conversation.

They told her all about their harrowing escape from North Korea. The only thing left out, they had no idea that the submarine had turned around to eliminate Room 39.

Alex promised to visit them again the next day.

David Fabio

She would continue her contact for the next month until she was sure the social worker had established good connections with them and the family was accepted by the neighborhood.

Duri Sol Ju's wife never heard from Duri again.

The last word she heard was what the Captain of the USS Cheyenne told her that he had been picked up by the police for stealing from the market.

U.S. intelligence confirmed reports that Duri Sol Ju was executed a month after his arrest in a mass execution designed to reduce the cost of keeping many of their political prisoners. It was also reported that Duri Sol Ju's co-worker was executed at the same time.

The report was classified "confidential" and never given to the family.

The successful results of Operation Blue caused massive changes in North Korea.

The lack of economy and the shutting down of their major sources of illegal funding by way of counterfeiting and internet schemes resulted in severe shortages in supplies throughout North Korea. Food rationing, shortages of clothing and fuel for power, greatly reduced all aspects of the government programs and caused severe problems for the people of the country.

The U.S. government is waiting to see what the final assessment of Operation Blue will do in reshaping relations with North Korea.

After the completion of Operation Blue, banks worldwide reported a serious reduction in counterfeit money detected within their systems.

It was hoped that it would stabilize the monetary systems in the U.S., Europe and China.

The Cyberwarfare operation in North Korea took a major hit by the malware planted by the U.S. An irony to North Korea holding corporations hostage by their malware, the worm released in their system did not have the option of allowing North Korea to pay to get their software back.

With their backup systems infected, North Korea tried to go into the black market to rebuild their systems. However, the black market software was much more detectable and did not have the sustainability to gather money like their original software.

It was believed it would take up to three years for them to rebuild their software system.

To the south, the nation of South Korea has started communications with the North in hopes of bringing stability to the region.

the end.

Author's Note:

I hope you enjoyed "The Ship."

This book started with two photographs I shot on a road trip with my wife. One included a ship with a bend in the middle.

When I watched the ship move back from the ore terminal in Two Harbors, I thought it was an illusion. Ships are not meant to bend in the middle.

The steel hull of ships are designed to uniformly flex slightly to prevent the stresses of high waves, or the loading of the ships, from cracking the keel and frame of the hull. Without this flexibility, once a critical stress is exceeded, the ship might break apart and sink to the bottom.

The photograph proved me wrong. This ship did bend in the middle. For the fiction storyline in the novel, I changed the name of the ship.

The other photograph was that of the dead badger on the side of the road. I was shooting wildlife photos when I spotted it. And yes, there was indeed a group of eagles picking it clean.

The photographs intrigued me. As I looked for some explanations for the photographs I shot that trip, I quickly realized there was a basis for a story hidden in the photos.

Someone once said a picture is worth a thousand words. For me, I would say an interesting picture is the start for a good story. In this case, one of puzzlement, as the story weaves into unexpected grounds.

Although the story in the novel is fiction, there are portions that may seem real to you. Recent stories in the news might depict similar situations.

I tried to keep the settings for the story as true as possible. The facts about the areas, and people involved, represent a close depiction.

With the controversies over North Korea, the historical facts are true. What may happen in the future in the country is yet to be seen. Could the disabling of Room 39 and their Cyberwarfare Center bring the North Korea economy to the point that the citizens and military might force the country to look for a new government? Who knows? In the early 1950's space travel was but a dream for fiction writers as well.

I hope you enjoyed the book. It was as fascinating to write, as it will be to read.

Enjoy!

David G. Fabio

Acknowledgements:

I would like to give special thanks to the following people. Without their help and direction, many of the facts in this novel would have never been known.

To my wife – Sandy; for putting up with the many hours of my working on the computer, as well as asking me to explain things in common terms.

To Kathleen Luhrsen and Jolene Chestnut; for their encouragement and suggestions for keeping the story accurate and on track.

About the Author

David Fabio is the author of two youth adventure novels – The Hidden Passage and The Second Summer.

He has also written a historical fiction novel for youth centered on life on the Mississippi River – Tales from a River's Bend.

Now, his seven other mystery novels – Search and Seizure, Secret of the Apostle Islands, Bayfield's Secret Notebook, Water Pressure, The Spot on the Wall, The Missing Jewels and Meadow House challenge the reader's imagination.

He is an educator, photographer, and an outdoor enthusiast. His love for nature and learning about the outdoors is evident in many of his writings.

Suggested other mysteries by the author:

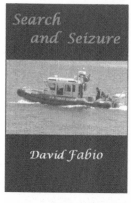

Search and Seizure – a suspense mystery about scientific research, espionage, and murder.

When a researcher is killed and another shanghaied, attempts to uncover the killer and solve the mystery by FBI Agent Lawson leads to unexpected places.

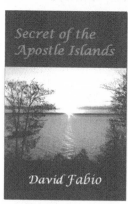

Secret of the Apostle Islands – the mystery of a lost sailboat, last seen in the Apostle Islands.

When a woman's husband goes missing, the story leads to adventure, romance, and intrigue in solving the case.

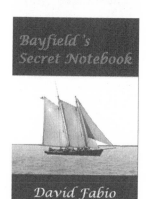

Bayfield's Secret Notebook – a historical fiction.

A long time hidden notebook is discovered that tells about its writer's involvement in the Confederacy's attempt to return gold to England at the end of the war.

The story leads from Kentucky to the Mississippi River, leading to Stillwater, Minnesota and eventually Bayfield, Wisconsin.

Water Pressure – when the state wants to pump water from Lake Superior to supply the major cities, because the rivers are contaminated, the mystery starts.

An international water conference leads to a murder mystery. It is up to Martin Berman and Tracy Saunders to follow up the leads given to their television stations along with the help of FBI Agent Mark Lawson.

This book involves mystery, romance and murder. Locations include: Minneapolis, St. Paul, Grand Marais, Duluth, Williston, and other towns.

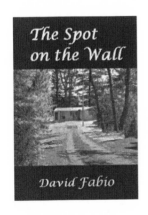

The Spot on the Wall – an action fiction.

When two old friends team up to work for a corporation that designs surveillance equipment, imaginations in technology go to work.

This book involves competition, imagination, high technology, mystery, kidnapping, and the FBI.

Located in Minnesota.

The Lost Jewels – an action fiction.

The a long lost relative's mysterious letter turns up talking about imminent danger and jewels, leading to a quest to solve the old mystery.

Locations include: Davenport Iowa, Kansas City Missouri, Alliance, North Platte and Kearney Nebraska

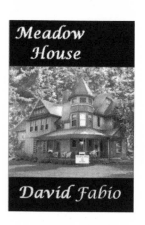

Meadow House – a historical fiction.

In the midst of a fictional story lies the interesting historical past of a small town in Minnesota – Marine on St. Croix. Why did a future President visit this community?

Locations include: Marine on St. Croix, St Cloud, and Stillwater, Minnesota.